IN
HARM'S
WAY

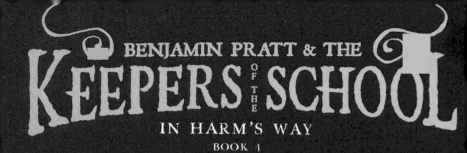

BENJAMIN PRATT & THE
KEEPERS OF THE SCHOOL

IN HARM'S WAY
BOOK 4

ANDREW CLEMENTS

ILLUSTRATED BY ADAM STOWER

Atheneum Books for Young Readers
New York London Toronto Sydney New Delhi

ATHENEUM BOOKS FOR YOUNG READERS

An imprint of Simon & Schuster Children's Publishing Division

1230 Avenue of the Americas, New York, New York 10020

For information about special discounts for bulk purchases, please contact Simon & Schuster Special Sales at 1-866-506-1949 or business@simonandschuster.com.

The Simon & Schuster Speakers Bureau can bring authors to your live event. For more information or to book an event, contact the Simon & Schuster Speakers Bureau at 1-866-248-3049 or visit our website at www.simonspeakers.com.

Book design by Sonia Chaghatzbanian

The text for this book is set in ITC Garamond Std.

The illustrations for this book are rendered in pen and ink.

Manufactured in the United States of America

0413 FFG

First Edition

10 9 8 7 6 5 4 3 2 1

Library of Congress Cataloging-in-Publication Data

Clements, Andrew, 1949–

In harm's way / Andrew Clements ; illustrated by Adam Stower. — First edition.

p cm. — (Benjamin Pratt & the Keepers of the School ; book 4)

Summary: As Benjamin Pratt and his friends Jill and Robert continue their efforts to save their school, they find themselves dodging two evil janitors, Lyman and Wally, but their team has also grown and now has a secret fund of millions of dollars.

ISBN 978-1-4169-3889-7

ISBN 978-1-4424-8145-9 (eBook)

[1. Mystery and detective stories. 2. Schools—Fiction. 3. Janitors—Fiction. 4. Sailing—Fiction. 5. Family life—Massachusetts—Fiction. 6. Massachusetts—Fiction.] I. Stower, Adam, illustrator. II. Title.

PZ7.C59118In 2013

[Fic]—dc23

2013001904

For Jeff and Janet Clements
—A. C.

IN
HARM'S
WAY

CHAPTER 1

Sneak Attack

"I want an explanation *now*!"

Benjamin Pratt stood in front of the principal's desk with Jill Acton and Robert Gerritt. Mr. Telmer had spotted them talking together in the hall before homeroom, and ordered them into his office.

And now they stared at the computer screen he had turned their way.

Mr. Telmer clicked the mouse, and they watched the video again: Three kids hurried along a dark hallway, their faces fuzzy in the red glow of an exit sign. The kids in the video looked a *lot* like them.

The principal had gotten an anonymous e-mail—a YouTube link to ten seconds of video with a dangerous title: "Pratt, Acton, and Gerritt Crash the School." The location was unmistakable: the first floor hallway near the office of the Captain Duncan Oakes School. And the time stamp on the video? May 30, 3:17 a.m., which was last Friday night—actually Saturday morning.

Ben forced his eyes to stay on the screen, afraid he would suddenly look up at the principal and shout, *Okay, we're guilty! Call the police! Bring the handcuffs!*

One thought looped through his mind.

We're dead! We are so dead! We're dead!

"Well?" growled Mr. Telmer. "What's going on here?"

From deep inside his private tunnel of fear, Ben thought he heard laughter.

Am I crazy?

He wasn't. Robert Gerritt was laughing.

Then Robert's voice: "Sorry, Mr. Telmer. I'm not being disrespectful, honest—I couldn't help it!"

Ben snapped fully alert as Robert kept talking.

"Because this looks like a huge prank, sir. Somebody used a phone camera to shoot three kids in the empty hallway . . . and changed the exposure so it would look like the middle of the night, and then added a fake time stamp, slapped *our* names on it, uploaded it to YouTube, and sent the link to your e-mail—which is right there on the school's website. That's what it looks like."

Mr. Telmer started to speak, but Robert didn't let him.

"And now, we're all here feeling sort of stupid. And, really, I'm sorry I laughed. I mean, I can't say where Jill was on Saturday at three thirty in the morning, but Ben and I were having a sleepover at my house—you can ask my mom. . . . I mean, my grandma . . . because . . ." Robert stopped dramatically and sniffed, and then sniffed again each time he paused. "Because . . . I live with Gram now . . . you know . . . because my mom and dad . . . aren't . . . you know, they're not . . . they're not *here* anymore!"

As Ben watched with a mixture of horror and

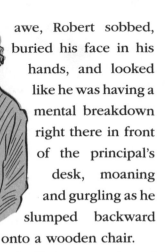

awe, Robert sobbed, buried his face in his hands, and looked like he was having a mental breakdown right there in front of the principal's desk, moaning and gurgling as he slumped backward onto a wooden chair.

Ben and Jill just stared, and Mr. Telmer didn't know what to do.

But he was the principal, so he had to do something. He hurried around the end of his desk and awkwardly patted Robert's shoulder.

"There, there . . . it's okay. I'm sure that this is just . . . a very bad joke. And I'm sorry it brought all . . . all that back for you. There, it's okay, Robert. Come, you should go now, all of you, go on to your homerooms . . . all right?"

As Robert got his sobbing under control, the principal helped him to his feet and handed him a couple of tissues from the box on his desk. Robert blew his nose while Mr. Telmer steered him out his door, through the main office, and into the hallway. Ben and Jill were close behind.

"Now, I want you kids to have a good day, all right? And let's just forget this happened. That's good . . . so . . . so have a great day!"

And with that, the principal hurried back into his office and shut the door.

Before they had walked ten feet, Robert had made a full recovery.

"Glad *that's* over," he muttered, then gave his nose one more blast.

Ben was still in shock. Because, what Robert had said about his mom and dad? That was true. They had died in a car crash when he was in kindergarten. But the way he had just used that terrible fact?

"Wow, Gerritt! You really . . . I mean . . . I mean, *wow*! That was just . . . *wow*!"

Jill was too shaken to be gushy. "Yeah, nice going, but that was a very close call!"

It was Monday morning. The front hallway was crowded with kids, but Ben felt like the three of them were the only ones there. And for sure, they *were* the only kids who knew that a war was raging inside this old building.

He scowled as they walked toward the south stairwell. It had been a bad weekend for the Keepers of the School. The kids on the YouTube video? That actually *was* Jill and Robert and him—inside the school at three thirty on Saturday morning. Illegally. They had just confirmed an important discovery under the stairs in the northwest corner—a secret Underground Railroad station, a discovery that should have permanently preserved the whole school and totally ended the Glennley Group's plans to build their new amusement park. But that creep Lyman had surprised them again, this time with a low-tech security device—a snarling Rottweiler named Moose. They had panicked, and they forgot to lock the secret door to the compartment, which is why the dog had been able to scratch his way in. So Lyman had found the hideout, realized what it was, and then his bosses at Glennley headquarters took over. In a huge rush, they had contacted all sorts of heritage and preservation groups. And late Saturday afternoon, the Glennley Group had issued a press release. They announced the discovery as if it were *theirs*, and made a promise to the world: They were going to keep this newly found Underground Railroad station just as it was, safe in its own small corner of the original school. But *most* of the old building was still going to be demolished to make room for their newest cheesy theme park, Tall Ships Ahoy!

On Sunday evening the school superintendent had held a press conference on the front steps of the Oakes School, and all the TV news stations from Boston had been there. Dr. Gill had smiled and smiled, talking into a cluster of microphones.

"I know I speak for the whole town of Edgeport when I say we are thrilled about this exciting discovery! The legacy of the Captain Duncan Oakes School will live on here forever, even though most of the building behind me will be gone."

When a reporter asked who had actually found the runaway slave hideout, the superintendent smiled again. "That person has chosen to remain anonymous so that the discovery itself can remain the center of attention."

So, thanks to Lyman and his dog, the big amusement park plans were still on track. In less than two weeks, the old school and the town of

Edgeport and its quiet harbor would be changed forever.

"That is not *happening!"*

"What?" asked Robert.

Ben realized he'd said that last bit out loud.

The three of them stopped near the doors to the south stairwell.

Ben talked through clenched teeth. "I *said,* Lyman and his sneaky lawyers and his nasty dog are *not* going to win!"

Robert grinned. "Of course not, Pratt. Relax! Look, I've gotta go check on something in the library before homeroom, but don't worry. I've got some ideas about the next safeguard, and how we are gonna spend some *serious* cash! Later." Gerritt took off toward the library.

Jill looked at Ben. "So, how did Lyman get that video of us?"

He shrugged. "Probably a motion-activated camera. But sending it to the principal? That's new. He wants to get us kicked out of school—or sent to jail. And his first shot was almost a direct hit."

The homeroom warning bell clanged three times.

Jill said, "Let's talk before math, okay? But don't take this stuff personally, Benjamin. That's partly why Lyman's so good—he's just doing his job. We can learn from him."

"Yeah," Ben said, "but can we beat him?"

"We have to," Jill said. "That's all—we have to." She gave him a half smile, then hit the stairs.

Ben walked toward the art room, which meant he had to go right past the door to the janitor's workshop. He was dreading an encounter with Lyman. The guy had stolen that whole Underground Railroad thing—a major victory. And now this new video attack, using the principal as a weapon? That was nasty . . . truly vicious. Like his Rottweiler.

Ben tapped his tongue against the back of his front teeth, a nervous habit. He really wanted to avoid Lyman. The guy was sure to give him one of those oily, sneering smiles.

The workroom was open, and just before he got there, Ben saw the end of the janitor's long trash cart come nosing out the doorway. He wanted to duck and slip past, but he couldn't help glancing left, straight into Lyman's face. And when he did that, he had to stop.

Ben stood there directly in front of the trash cart, heart pounding, almost in a trance.

The man shot him a dark, angry look.

"Move it, Pratt!"

Ben jumped aside, but he kept staring at the janitor.

It wasn't Lyman.

CHAPTER 2

The Times that Try

What?!

Ben stood there, trying to process what he was seeing.

A short, stocky man in a green janitor's uniform pushed the trash cart down the hall toward the office.

He's *the janitor now? But where's Lyman?*

Another thought slammed into his head.

I've never seen that guy

before, and he said my name—*he knew my face!*

Only one possibility: Lyman must have given that man his picture—probably Jill's and Robert's, too. Plus their class schedules, home addresses, cell phone numbers—probably a complete file on each of them!

Ben clenched his teeth so hard they hurt.

The clock in his head told him the final homeroom bell was about to clang, and he couldn't be late—that would mean detention. He wheeled around and hurried toward the art room, staring down at the wooden floor, lost in thought.

So . . . where's Lyman? Is this guy his replacement? Or maybe . . .

"Good morning, young fella."

Ben gulped.

Lyman's bony fingers were wrapped around the wooden handle of a dust mop. He stood beside the art room door, wearing that crooked, sneering smile. As he spoke, his smile got wider.

"Saw you met my new assistant. Wally has *skills*. The YouTube thing? That was all Wally. I sure hope you and your little pals didn't get in any trouble this morning."

Ben shivered, couldn't help it. He had stood

face-to-face with Lyman for the first time fourteen days ago, and he felt the same way now—hypnotized, like a mouse staring up at a snake, about to be swallowed alive.

The first clang of the final bell snapped him out of it, and he took two quick steps into the art room—*not* tardy.

And he felt safer, too. A bolt of anger flashed through his heart, and Ben saw the perfect way to direct it.

"Isn't that nice!" he said, oozing sarcasm. "We all have a new friend to play with!" He looked up into those dark, deep-set eyes, and now Ben was smiling too. "So . . . I guess this means that good old Jerry Lyman couldn't handle this job on his own—*right*?"

Lyman's upper lip curled into a snarl, and Ben's smile grew broader. "Well, gotta go to school now, Mr. Lyman—and I hope you and your little pal Wally have a *wonderful* day, okay?"

He turned and walked quickly to a table near the front of the art room. Ben was sure the man was still glaring at him, but he didn't look back. Lyman could stand there ten years for all he cared!

Ms. Wilton began taking attendance, and Ben felt so happy, he could have floated up out of his chair. Getting the last word with Lyman? Sweet! But this feeling was more than that.

Because what he'd said to the man was true: *Someone* had decided that Jerroald Lyman, a highly trained, fully equipped industrial spy, was not able to deal with a few sixth graders at the Captain Oakes School. And therefore, a decision had been made over the weekend: Send reinforcements to the front lines.

And *that* was a compliment! And—

Whoa! Whoa, whoa, whoa. Wait a minute! The school superintendent? She must know that Lyman works for Glennley—she has to!

How else could Lyman's buddy suddenly show up on a Monday morning as a new school employee?

And . . . the principal must be totally in the dark about everything! Otherwise, Mr. Telmer wouldn't have let them off the hook about that video. . . .

So many layers to this thing!

Ben glanced around. Lyman had left, and Ms. Wilton was busy prepping for first period.

He got out his phone and tapped a text to Jill and Robert.

Lyman has reinforcements—
Wally the junior janitor.
Beware!

Ben sent the message and then stared out the window, replaying what he'd said to Lyman. He wasn't sorry about that, not one bit.

Jill always said they should avoid all contact with Lyman. And she said never to take any of this stuff personally.

But it *was* personal.

And the look on Lyman's face when he'd said that about not being able to handle the work? Beautiful!

Maybe if he got Lyman mad enough, it might actually help. Angry people make mistakes. . . .

Still staring out the window, Ben could see the top of the copper beech tree on the south lawn of the school. It towered above the oaks and maples, swaying with the onshore breeze. That massive tree had survived every hurricane and nor'easter for more than a hundred and fifty years.

And so had the Oakes school. Except the

roots of the school went even deeper. They'd been growing into the heart of this town since before the US Constitution was written. Captain Oakes had planned it so his school would overlook the ocean, and he'd left the building and the land for the children and families of Edgeport. It was something good, and it was meant to be permanent.

And it's gonna take more than Lyman and his sidekick to knock it down!

Ben caught himself—it felt like he was bragging, and he hated that.

But then he decided he was just giving himself a pep talk. Which was fine. Right about now, he needed all the encouragement he could muster.

A quote popped into his mind, something Thomas Paine had written in 1776, part of the most famous pep talk of the American Revolution: "These are the times that try men's souls. The summer soldier and the sunshine patriot will, in this crisis, shrink from the service of their country; but he that stands by it now, deserves the love and thanks of man and woman."

Except I'm not looking for thanks . . . or love, either.

At this point, the Keepers had serious choices to make. They had to take the battle to the enemy. They had to use every advantage they could grab, and they had to make every day count—every minute. And if Lyman and Wally got nasty, they'd just have to deal with it.

Most of all, they couldn't give up. He and Jill and Robert were being tried in ways they hadn't imagined, being tested over and over again. And if they failed, the whole town of Edgeport would be different forever.

No . . . not just different—ruined!

The demand of *this* crisis was clear: It was time to stand and fight.

CHAPTER 3

The Score

On his way to first period, Ben saw Wally again.

And Wally saw Ben see him.

Then Ben saw that Wally *wanted* to be seen. He was directly across the hall from the music room, the new assistant thug, standing guard along the south side of the school.

Ben felt the urge to smile and wave at him, but he controlled it. He slipped into the music room and took his place in the tenor section of the chorus, a spot where he couldn't be observed through the open doorway.

Even after almost two weeks, it still bothered him, being watched all the time. But, then again, it was another compliment. Lyman and Wally were admitting that they needed to keep a close watch on the Keepers. After all, if it hadn't been for Lyman's dog, their discovery last week might have shut down the whole Glennley scheme.

So the Glennley operatives knew the kids had to be kept from doing more searching. But the good part? Lyman had no idea *why* they were searching in the first place.

Ben smiled to himself. Lyman knew *nothing* about the careful plans Captain Oakes had made almost three centuries ago—plans that were now Ben's responsibility.

For the past eighteen days, he'd been on a treasure hunt—actually, a safeguard hunt. And the hunt had been successful, too, right under Lyman's nose.

Because back in 1783, Captain Oakes had looked into the future. He'd felt sure that some day, someone would want this beautiful oceanfront land and would try to take it away from the children and families of Edgeport. And therefore, he had placed things around the school, hidden safeguards that he hoped would help future Keepers defend his school—his life's most important accomplishment.

And Ben knew they had made good progress.

The bell clanged, and he opened his music book. The chorus was rehearsing songs for the final concert. It was called An American Songfest, and it was going to be a last farewell to the old school.

Mr. Maasen played a loud chord on his piano, which brought the group to order, and they started in with "Yankee Doodle."

Ben sang, but only with his mouth. His mind was busy ticking through the safeguard clues. He knew them by heart:

After five bells sound, time to sit down.
After four times four, tread up one more.
After three hooks pass, one will be brass.
After two tides spin, a man walks in.
After one still star, horizons afar.

The "five bells" clue had helped them find an addition to Captain Oakes's original will, a codicil. It was one sheet of parchment in the captain's own handwriting, but whoever took that simple document to the courthouse instantly became the new owner of the school and the twenty acres around it. However, if the Keepers actually *did* that, then this war would become a purely legal battle, which seemed risky: The Glennley Group had a battalion of tough lawyers. Jill and Ben had decided to use the codicil only as a last resort.

The second clue, "tread up one more," had led to a secret space under a staircase—actually, *two* secret spaces. Under the north stairwell was where they'd found the Underground Railway station—but, of course, that hadn't been planned in 1783.

The actual safeguard was a brass token hidden below the south staircase, a token which gave them access to an account at the Edgeport Bank and Trust Company. The captain's original deposit of about fourteen thousand dollars worth of gold had been tended carefully by the bank for more than two hundred and ten years, and last Thursday the Keepers had learned that they now had a secret fund that they could use "for the welfare, preservation, and continuing operation of the Captain Duncan Oakes School." The fund was truly massive, over eighty-eight million dollars! And Lyman and his bosses knew nothing about it.

Another recent advantage? They had been joined by two grown-ups. Mrs. Keane was the wife of the *real* school janitor, the man who had recruited Ben to be the new Keeper—just before he died. Then, at Mr. Keane's funeral, Ben had met Tom Benton, who had been the janitor at Oakes School before Mr. Keane took over from him.

And Robert Gerritt was a Keeper too—which would never have happened if Jill hadn't forced the issue. Ben now had to admit that Robert's intelligence was remarkable. But his personality? Sometimes hard to take. . . . Very.

So, now they had five official Keepers, a huge reserve of cash, and a secret list with three more clues—good, solid resources.

And they also had keys to every door in the school, thanks to Mrs. Keane. They were her husband's keys, and they'd already been useful— that was how they had gotten inside the school at three in the morning on Saturday.

But what they did *not* have was time. The school was scheduled for demolition on June 11, right after school let out for the summer—in just ten days.

They had to get that next safeguard, but first

they had to crack a new clue: *After three hooks pass, one will be brass.*

Gerritt said he had ideas. Which was good. The guy was a genuine genius—and Ben had no trouble admitting that . . . most of the time.

Robert could still be incredibly obnoxious and pushy and annoying, but those flashes of pure brilliance? They made up for the other stuff . . . most of the time.

After "Yankee Doodle" the chorus moved on to an old sea chantey. And when they sang, "Hey, haul away, we're bound for better weather," Ben had to smile. Because last week had also brought him a surprise—a sailboat, his very own Optimist. He still couldn't believe it. The boat wasn't *totally* new, but the sails and rigging were, and the hull was smooth and clean.

He couldn't wait to face off against Gerritt. They belonged to the same sailing club and had fought for first place in their division all last season. Working together at school didn't mean they had to play nice out on the water. This Saturday's race was going to be epic!

And the best thing about the new boat? His mom and dad had teamed up to get it for him—

the first thing they'd really done together since their separation two months ago.

Ben loved the next song, and threw his heart and soul into the first lines: "I've been working on the railroad, all the live long day . . ."

But his thoughts quickly wandered again.

The Underground Railroad thing? That must have really scared the Glennley people. And Lyman and Wally were going to do everything they could to shut off any more searching, any other bit of free time that he and Jill and Robert had inside the school.

Of course, their social studies project gave them an edge. They had special permission from Mrs. Hinman and the librarian to arrive early and stay late to do research about the history of the school.

Their base camp for the project was the library, and Lyman had been doing his best to keep them bottled up in there—and failing.

But with Lyman on super high alert, and now Wally too? If they were going to make any progress, they'd need new strategies.

After three hooks pass, one will be brass.

Hooks . . . what kind of hooks? He had started

a list, but nothing made sense yet. Maybe it was something to do with the carvings. . . .

The intercom speaker crackled, and there was one clang, about half as loud as a normal bell. As the singing stopped, the voice of the school secretary filled the music room. "Mr. Maasen? Please send Benjamin Pratt to the office right away. He has an emergency phone call."

CHAPTER 4

Thumping

Ben stood frozen for two seconds, but when the intercom message sank in, he scrambled off the risers, dropped his music notebook, grabbed his book bag, and rushed out of the music room. He almost sprinted through the halls.

Emergency?

The worst possible fears filled his mind—this had to be about his mom or dad, didn't it? Something bad . . . something awful!

He burst into the office, and Mrs. Hendon pointed him toward the nurse's room.

"There's no one in there, Ben. Push the button

for line three. Here, I'll close the door so you have some privacy."

Ben was breathing hard, almost felt faint. His fingers were cold and shaky, and he had trouble hitting the blinking button on the phone.

"H-hello?"

"Who am I speaking with?" A man's voice, very official.

Almost in a whisper Ben said, "This is Benjamin Pratt."

"Hey, Pratt, glad you made it. Listen, I need—"

"Wh-what? Who is this?" Ben shook his head like he'd just been punched.

"Relax, Pratt, it's me, Gerritt. I'm calling from the boys' room up on the third floor—don't have much time. I need you to—"

"You are such a *jerk*, Gerritt! I thought my mom or dad—"

"Yeah, I know, I know. Sorry about that, but I had to get you out of class quick so you could check on something, and I didn't want Stretch and Stumpy to be—"

"Who?"

"Lyman and Wally—I met the little guy on my way out of the library before homeroom—looks like a gnome. Anyway, the evil twins think you're in chorus now, right? I mean, like, they didn't see you in the hall on your way to the office, did they?"

"No, I don't think so. . . ." Ben felt dazed, but Robert pushed ahead.

"Great, so listen up. I need you to do something. You know the tall curved posts along the outer walls in the east-west hallways, the ones that hold up the ceiling beams?"

"Yeah . . ."

"Well, I need you to thump on each one of them."

"What—*why*?" said Ben.

"No time to explain, just do it. And hit 'em with something hard."

"Like what?"

"Like your head, Pratt—I don't know, find something hard, anything. And when you thump, listen."

"Listen?"

"Yeah, you have to *listen*, and pay attention. I'll quiz you later. Gotta go."

"Hey, w-wait!" Ben spluttered. "What am I supposed to say to the school secretary about this?"

"About what?"

"About this phone call, idiot—what do I tell her?"

Robert laughed. "How should I know? *You're* the one with the emergency! See you later."

The line went dead.

Ben hung up and went back into the office. The secretary hurried over.

"Anything I can help with, dear?"

Ben shook his head. "Um, actually . . . everything's okay now. This guy . . . at my mom's office? He got worried because she was really late for work . . . for a meeting . . . and she wasn't answering her phone, and he thought there might have been some kind of trouble . . . and he didn't know how to get hold of my dad. But my mom got there when we were talking . . . some kind of car trouble. Um . . . could I have a pass back to music?"

Ben was furious at Gerritt for forcing him to do this—he hated having to lie. But Mrs. Hendon looked so relieved, Ben was afraid she might try to hug him.

She was all smiles as she filled out the hall pass. "I am so *glad* it turned out to be nothing! Here you are, Benjamin."

Ben suddenly knew what he could use to

thump the beams. He'd found a baseball in the gutter along Washington Street about two weeks ago, pretty scuffed up, but not terrible. And it was still in the bottom of his book bag.

He turned left outside the office, and then reached into his backpack and found the hardball. The first upright was near the corner, before the south stairwell doors.

He looked to be sure the coast was clear, then held the baseball tightly in his palm and gave the dark oak post a good whack.

Thunk.

The hallway was empty, but that could change any second. He hurried to the next post.

Thunk.

The third post was right before the door to the janitor's workroom, so Ben hit it with a little less force.

Thunk—same sound.

Neither of the men was in the workshop— what had Robert called them? Oh yeah—Stretch and Stumpy. Pretty funny.

He hit the fourth post.

Thunk—the same solid, deep sound, like hitting a tree.

He was beginning to feel pretty stupid, and he was getting madder at Gerritt with every step, ready to quit. He looked ahead, counted seven more posts, and decided he'd at least finish this side of the school before going back to chorus. He picked up the pace.

Just as he was thumping the sixth post, Luke Barton came out of the boys' room.

Thunk.

The kid smiled and walked over. "What're you doing?"

"What's it look like I'm doing?"
Ben walked quickly to the next post.
Thunk.

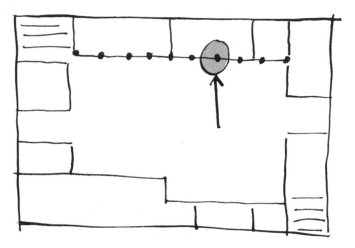

Luke stuck with him. "Can I do the next one?"

"Sure," said Ben. "But if you get caught, don't blame me."

He tossed him the ball, and Luke ran to the next post and really whomped it.

Thunk.

He turned to Ben and grinned. "Cool!"

Ben did not see anything even a little bit cool about hitting a wooden post with a scuffed baseball, but he nodded and said, "Yeah, cool."

Luke tossed the ball back.

"Thanks, Pratt. See you later."

"Yup."

Ben walked casually to the next post, and without even breaking his stride, he gave it a glancing blow with the ball.

He stopped.

Retracing two steps, he stood facing the post.

He tilted his head. Was that a *thunk*?

He looked both ways. Luke had rounded the corner, and the hallway was empty again.

He reached back and slammed the hardball against the post.

Not much like a *thunk*.

He hit it once more, and this time he was sure.

This post had a sound all its own.

CHAPTER 5

Hooked

"You're absolutely sure?"

"Yes, Gerritt, I'm sure. I know the difference between a *thunk* and a *bong*. Go hit the post yourself. The eighth one from the south stairwell goes *bong*."

Ben took a bite of chocolate cake. He could tell from the shape of Robert's eyebrows that the quiz wasn't over.

He and Jill and Robert were back in a corner of the cafeteria where they'd never eaten before. They ate lunch in a different spot every day now, so Lyman wouldn't know where to plant a listening device. Ben wished he could eat in peace, but every lunchtime ended up being a war council.

"So . . . this *bong*," said Gerritt. "Is the tone high or low?"

"Low. Definitely low." Ben took a long pull on the straw in his milk carton. His cake was gone, which meant he had to start in on the grilled cheese and salad. Always a sad moment.

"And is the sound solid, or is it more of a hollow sound?"

"Hmm . . ." Ben bit off a chunk of sandwich, chewed slowly, then swallowed, and took a sip of milk. "I'd say there's some of each. The sound itself is pretty solid, but there's a little bit of echo in there too. Like a gong—which rhymes with *bong*."

Jill was done eating and held up her hand to interrupt before the quiz could continue. "Enough with the suspense, Robert. What's all this about?"

"Simple: It's about hooks. From the next clue, right? 'After three hooks pass,' and all that. I started a list last night, every kind of hook I could think of."

"I did that too," Ben said.

"So did I," said Jill.

36

"Okay," Robert said, "how many different kinds did you guys come up with?"

Ben said, "Coat hooks, cup hooks, grappling hooks, boat hooks, button hooks, fish hooks—"

Jill jumped in. "And iron pot hooks, for hanging pots in a fireplace. And picture hooks, chain hooks, meat hooks, like, in a butcher shop. And a weed hook, which is another name for a sickle—"

"And also door or window hooks," said Ben, "like for screens."

"Or a hook to replace a hand, like Captain Hook had in *Peter Pan* . . ."

Robert nodded. "Yeah, I got all those, and some other ones, too. And none of them seemed to connect with what we know about the school. But *then*, I started thinking like John Vining."

Ben knew that name—they all did. John Vining was a ship's carpenter, the man Captain Oakes had hired back in the 1780s to transform his huge brick warehouse into a school. Vining was also the person who must have figured out how to hide the safeguards.

Ben smiled as he chewed another bite of sandwich. Robert was about to show them how smart he was. Again. And since he was now able to feel less jealous and less annoyed about that, Ben was ready to be entertained.

Turning to Jill, Robert said, "Remember the name they used for the third floor of the school, on that coin Mr. Keane gave to Pratt?"

Jill nodded. "'The upper deck.'"

"Exactly," said Robert, "which is a shipbuilding term *applied* to the school building." Looking at Ben, he said, "And what did they call the exact center of the school?"

"'Amidships.'"

"Right—a nautical term. And that's why it seemed logical that the word 'hooks' in this clue could also have some kind of nautical meaning, something to do with the way ships are built or described. So, I accessed the online *Oxford English Dictionary* through the Edgeport Public Library, and I did a Boolean search, and—"

"A *what*?" said Jill.

"A Boolean search—named after George Boole, a math guy. I wanted to find all the connections in the whole history of the English language between shipbuilding and the word 'hook,' so I asked the *OED* to search for 'ship AND hook,' with that word 'AND' in all capital letters. And when you search that way, it finds any definitions that include *both* those terms. And the dictionary found me a word: 'futtock.'"

"What?" said Ben.

"Futtock," Robert said. "It rhymes with 'buttock.'"

"Lovely," said Jill. "And what does this word that rhymes with 'buttock' have to do with posts in the hallway which make different sounds when poor Benjamin goes sneaking around hitting them with a baseball?"

As usual, Robert wasn't going to be hurried. Ben used his napkin to hide his smile. He wasn't sure which was more fun—Robert showing off his smarts, or Jill getting impatient about it.

"I'll explain in a second. So, the *OED* is a *fantastic* research tool. A little more reading inside the definition revealed that this word 'futtock' is a combination of two words that sailors said together quickly: 'foot-hook'—that's right, *hook*! And to explain *that*, the *OED* quoted from a very old book about ship construction, written in 1611 by Captain John Smith."

Ben leaned forward. "Really? The same guy who was saved by Pocahontas?"

Robert nodded and pulled a scrap of paper out of his pocket. "Yup, and Smith's book, called *The Seaman's Grammar*, says 'Your rising timbers are the hookes, or ground timbers and foot-hookes placed on the keel.' So, if Captain Oakes and John Vining are using that word with this nautical meaning, and they apply it to this *building*, what would those hooks be?" Robert quickly answered his own question. "Those big curved posts in the halls! And to seal the deal, this morning I checked in the rare books section of our library, and I

found a copy of that very book by John Smith—
with John Vining's name written in it!"

Ben said, "And you wanted me to hit the posts
to see if any *didn't* sound like wood."

"Exactly. 'After three hooks pass, one will be
brass.' And *bong* is a brass sound."

Ben was about to say that the count wasn't
right, but he saw his mistake.

"Oh . . . if you start counting at the post closest
to the art room, then the post that goes *bong* is
the fourth one—it all fits!" Ben had to grin. "That
is very cool, Gerritt! *Very!*"

Jill smiled in agreement, but immediately said,
"Still, it's not like that solves the clue. And how
come you couldn't just look at the post and *see* it
was made of metal instead of wood?"

Robert said, "I'm guessing that the post was
painted carefully to look like wood, or else there's
a thin layer of wood glued on top of the brass,
a veneer. And you're right—we haven't solved
anything yet. But at least we know where to start
looking."

Jill scowled. "It's not much help that the post
is right out there in the hallway, and pretty close
to the janitor's room, too."

"Which is why," Robert said, "we need a really excellent camera."

Ben nodded. "Sure, snap some pix, and we can study the post without having to stand there staring at it."

"So . . . we all agree? 'Cause I located this sweet little camera with a great lens and huge megapixels—and Tom Benton could get it from Ace Camera so we'll have it by tomorrow!"

Ben saw Jill start to frown. She didn't like how Robert always took charge, or the way he had started talking about spending money the minute they learned about their superfund. Ben was expecting a sharp word or two, but suddenly her face softened.

"I vote yes," she said. "Get the best camera you can. That pile of money is probably our most powerful weapon, so let's *use* it!"

Robert grinned. "All *right*! Because I've got other ideas about tools and equipment, and some weapon systems, and it's gonna take some real cash, so this is—"

He stopped talking, and Ben saw his eyes get wide. Robert's smile vanished.

"Incoming!" he whispered. "It's Wally, twenty

feet away and closing in fast. You know what to do!"

Without another word, all three of them stood up, grabbed their things, walked quickly to the corner, and dropped off their lunch trays. Jill immediately headed out the west door onto the playground, and Robert left the cafeteria through the door that went into the Annex, the newer one-story part of the school.

That left Ben alone in the lunchroom, but he didn't leave right away. He walked back to a table and sat down across from Luke and Bill.

"Hey guys, how's it going?"

He smiled at them when they replied, but he barely heard them. He was watching Wally out of the corner of his eye.

The man was lousy at pretending to be a janitor. He was still back near the corner where they'd been eating, shoving his mop around in a circle. Wally was watching Ben, but his eyes kept darting to the doors where Jill and Robert had disappeared. He had been given the job of tracking the Keepers during lunch, and now two-thirds of them were missing.

Ben said, "That science quiz on Friday was tough, didn't you think?" He acted like he was totally into a conversation with the two guys, and in less than fifteen seconds, it happened. Wally bolted toward the door Robert had used, and when he got there, he leaned his mop up against the wall, took one more quick glance at Ben, and then trotted out into the hallway.

The second he disappeared, Ben said, "Well, guys, gotta go!"

He was halfway through the door that led toward the old building when Mrs. Flagg stopped him.

"Do you have a hall pass?"

Ben wanted to shout, *What is your* problem, *lady? You* know *I have a pass—I've been showing it to you every day after lunch for two weeks!*

But he didn't yell. He smiled sweetly and handed her the worn slip of bright yellow paper that both Mrs. Hinman and Mrs. Sinclair had signed.

"All right, you may go," she said.

Ben bounced into the causeway and walked as fast as he dared, glancing back once to see if Wally was following. He wasn't.

Which was good. Because Ben needed to make a quick trip to the office—that was the whole point of their sudden three-way split at lunch. And he got there in less than two minutes, with no sign of either janitor.

The school secretary looked up and then smiled at him.

Ben smiled back. "Hi, Mrs. Hendon. At lunch I noticed there's a new janitor. I'd like to interview him for that project we're doing on the school's history—ask him about his first impressions of the old building. Can you tell me his whole name? I mean, I don't want to walk up and have to call him 'Mister Janitor' or something."

Mrs. Hendon nodded and started looking through a stack of papers. "He's brand new in town, and I just got his paperwork this morning—although why they're hiring someone at this time of year is beyond me. All right, here it is. His name is Wallace V. Robleton." And then she spelled out the last name.

"Great," Ben said. "Thanks! Well, see you later."

Ben left the office and turned toward the library. Mission accomplished! He couldn't help smiling—he loved this spy stuff.

He was also happy that the name wasn't something common. With a name like Wallace V.

Robleton, they could probably find out something about him on the Internet, maybe something useful. There was no telling what a careful search might turn up.

Ben had read a lot of history about real wars, and spying was always important—it was called intelligence gathering. To win a war, you had to learn as much as possible about your enemy.

Even if his nickname was Stumpy.

CHAPTER 6

Game Changer

Walking out of the school late Monday afternoon, Ben felt a big wave of relief.

Is this how a soldier feels when he leaves the battlefield and goes home?

But then he remembered that his life hadn't been in danger today, not like a real soldier in a bombs-and-bullets war. But there were some similarities. . . .

For one thing, there were certainly two opposing sides here, each with a different vision of what the outcome of this fight should be.

And that thing this morning with the principal and the video? That had been a real attack that could have hurt them—but not physically . . . not unless you count being grounded all summer as a life-threatening problem.

No, this wasn't much like an armed conflict. This was more a war of ideas. And if he and the other Keepers were going to win it, they were going to have to outthink the Glennley goons.

Ben thought about that and decided there was some good progress in that area. Because as the war had progressed, their small army of Keepers had become a group of specialists.

Robert had quickly established himself as the master strategist. He was just so smart! Which was good thing . . . about 99 percent of the time. Ingenious tactics, brilliant plans, clever diversions, even a nonlethal weapons engineer—he was just . . . smart.

And Jill had become the great questioner, the one who kept pushing everyone to do their best thinking. Plus she was a whiz at Internet research— she was the one assigned to explore the world of Wallace V. Robleton tonight. And she was the one who was always ready with encouragement, always able to see a way out, a next step. Well . . . almost always. And she was fearless—she was the one who had demanded that they recruit Robert, a gutsy move which had turned out to be a great decision . . . about 99 percent of the time.

Tom Benton, the retired janitor? He had become the treasurer and supplies expert. It had been his idea to set up a credit card linked to the huge Oakes trust fund so they wouldn't have to rush over to Edgeport Bank and Trust every time the Keepers needed to buy something. At this very moment, he was busy ordering and assembling all the equipment Robert had selected.

Mrs. Keane wasn't involved very much, not yet . . . but her husband's keys certainly were. Plus she made the best chocolate cake in the known universe—an important morale booster!

But what's my specialty? Whacking wooden posts with a hardball?

Ben shrugged off that thought and looked both ways before he crossed Central Street and headed west toward home.

One of my homes . . .

Since his parents had separated, he'd been living in two places—one week with his dad on their sailboat at Parson's Marina, and the next week with his mom at the family house on Walnut Street.

He shook his head and made himself push all that out of his mind. He had to stay focused on the business at hand.

The afternoon had been mostly school as usual—with constant surveillance courtesy of Stretch and Stumpy. And the time in the library after school today had been especially frustrating.

Lyman used to have one big weakness—he had to keep doing all the school custodial work, even though his real job was to protect the interests of his bosses at Glennley. So whenever he got busy elsewhere in the school, the Keepers had been able to search for that next safeguard, the one that might help win the war.

But Wally's presence had changed all that, and this afternoon had been their first real taste of it. While Lyman had kept up his disguise, doing the real janitorial duties, Wally had stayed close to the library, just pretending to work.

The best moment of today's after school session had been when Ben and Jill and Robert staged another split-up like the one they'd done at lunch. All three of them suddenly left the library and headed off in different directions.

But even that hadn't been very effective. Wally

and Lyman were using walkie-talkies now, and as Ben left the library, he'd heard Wally say into the microphone clipped to his collar, "Unit one is headed for the south stairs, unit three is going toward the office, and unit two is in sight."

Lyman had replied instantly, "I'm on it. Stick with unit two!"

When Ben—unit three—came around the corner near the office, there was Lyman, standing at the far corner where he could watch both long hallways at once, a good observation point.

Completely ignoring him, Ben went trotting past and started up the north stairs, so Lyman had to make a choice—and he did. He followed, and Ben heard his boots pounding along behind him, all the way up to the third floor, then around the hallway to the south stairs, down to the second floor, back around to the north stairs, down to the first floor, and then left, taking the long way around the first-floor hallway back to the library again. And during that time when Lyman was following him and Wally was following Jill, unit two, Robert, was on his own.

But that was only for about three minutes, barely enough time for Robert to examine the hallway near the art room. He was checking to see if Wally had hidden any small cameras, like the one that had captured their three a.m. visit to the school over the weekend. He didn't spot any, but that didn't mean the cameras weren't there . . . three minutes wasn't much search time.

No, there was no doubt about it: Wally was a game changer.

Ben was about three driveways from his house on Walnut Street when he heard a car coming up behind him, and then a horn tooted. He turned to look and saw a small car, dark green. And Wally was driving.

His head barely rose above the level of the steering wheel, and the passenger window was rolled down. He tooted his horn once more, waved and smiled, then gunned the engine and sped away down the block.

Well, that's creepy, Ben thought.

But just as quickly, he shrugged it off. So what? Of course they knew where he lived. And of course they would want to know where he was after school. And now that Glennley had doubled the size of its local army, all the Keepers could expect more pressure, more aggressive tracking.

And why had Wally honked and waved? He wanted Ben to *know* he was being tracked, that the fight was on. And that the battlefield didn't begin or end at the doors of the school—not that it ever had, not really. After all, Lyman had snooped around at his dad's boat over two weeks ago, pretending to be a yacht broker.

Before Ben even put the key in the kitchen door, Nelson was barking and scratching on the other side. And when the door opened, the corgi came bursting out onto the driveway, running circles around him and yipping like a puppy. Coming home to Nelson was a lot better than walking to the marina and hanging out on the empty sailboat until his dad got home.

But neither of his parents usually worked late. His mom worked as a real estate agent, so her hours were pretty flexible. He looked at the clock—four forty-five. Mom would be home in an hour or so.

And soon his dad would be off for the summer—Beecham High School was on the same schedule as the Edgeport schools . . . or was he planning to teach geometry at summer school, or that lacrosse camp? Ben wasn't sure.

Before the separation, the big plan for this

summer had been a family cruise on the *Tempus Fugit*, somewhere south—maybe even the Bahamas. It wasn't happening, not this summer. Maybe not ever.

Again, he pushed his own worries away.

I should go up and do some homework.

But the thought of climbing the stairs all the way up to his attic bedroom stopped him cold, right in front of the family-room couch. He shrugged off his backpack and flopped onto the pillows.

He stretched out and yawned, and the corgi immediately jumped up beside him. Staring up at the ceiling, Ben reached down and scratched behind Nelson's ears. The dog snuggled closer.

It was so peaceful here. So unlike being at school. And unlike the sailboat, too—everything perfectly still. And quiet.

What do they call this in the army?

He couldn't recall, so he closed his eyes and stopped trying. And then it came to him.

Right . . . R & R. I'm getting a little R & R—rest and relaxation.

In less than a minute, the soldier and his dog were asleep.

CHAPTER 7

Divide and Conquer

"Nelson, get *down* off that couch!"

The corgi yelped, and all four of his short little legs kicked into overdrive as he dove to the floor and scrambled for cover.

Ben sat up, dazed and bleary-eyed.

"Benjamin, you know that dog is *not* allowed on the furniture!"

"Right . . . guess I fell asleep."

"Well, get up and plump those cushions, and help me get this room presentable. And get

Nelson's toys put away too. And then take your things up to your room."

His mom was bustling around, gathering up books and newspapers, and wiping dust off the end tables with a cloth.

"I've got a client coming here for a meeting in five minutes—so dinner might be a little late. Did you get a snack? Maybe we'll order some Chinese. Come on now, get off the couch and help me out, move it!"

R & R was definitely over.

Ben did all he'd been ordered to and then trudged up to his room. He sat down at his laptop and checked his e-mail—nothing. He was hoping to hear what Jill had dug up about Wallace V. Robleton, but she probably hadn't even started searching yet.

He closed the computer and almost lay down on his bed—he still felt groggy. But then the doorbell rang, and now he was too hungry to nap anyway. Time for that snack.

He walked quietly down to the first floor, and at the bottom of the stairs he turned right and went to the kitchen.

The visitor was a man with a strong, deep voice.

"Well, we've heard so much about your work here in Edgeport—it's a pleasure to meet you."

Ben smiled. His mom was a great real estate agent—she worked really hard at it, and she loved helping people.

He tried to sneak to the refrigerator—all he really wanted was a cold glass of milk. Chinese food in a little while . . . that sounded so good.

His mom noticed him through the doorway, and so did the visitor.

"And is this young man your son? Of course he is—I can see it in his face!"

"Ben," his mom said, "come and meet Mr. Birch."

The man stood up as Ben came into the room. Ben held out his hand, gave a good strong grip, and looked the man in the eye as they shook, just like his dad had taught him to. "Pleased to meet you."

The man held on to his hand. "Pleased to meet you too, Ben. And I'm glad to say that I'm here on a very happy mission—I have been authorized to make your mom a very rich woman. Would you like that?"

Ben smiled awkwardly and began to relax his hand and back away, but the man gripped it even tighter, almost too tightly. Almost hurting.

"Yes sir, Ben, you're mom is going to be a *very* rich woman!"

Ben pulled his hand away, confused.

"Why don't you tell Ben what we've been talking about, Bonnie?"

Ben didn't like the way he used his mom's first

name like that. It was too familiar. But his mom seemed flattered.

"Well, it's a little complicated, but Mr. Birch represents a company that has been buying up properties both north and south of Edgeport harbor for the past year, and they have plans for some very nice, very tasteful low-rise condominiums."

The man winked at Ben. "Strictly classy places—with *big* price tags! And tell him how many units we plan to lay on, Bonnie."

"Between four and five hundred new units over the next three years, and they've asked me to be the exclusive listing broker for all of them! Isn't that wonderful?"

"Um, yeah . . . that's great," said Ben.

He knew a little about his mom's business and started running the math in his head. As the listing broker, she would probably get about 3 percent of every sale . . . and if there were four hundred units, and if each one sold for, say, two hundred thousand dollars . . . then this offer was worth . . . close to three million dollars, maybe more!

So, yeah, it was a *very* big deal.

Mr. Birch cleared his throat. "Of course, this all depends on that new theme park, Tall Ships

Ahoy! We've been buying property that's far enough away so the park'll just be a pleasant blur of pretty lights on the waters of the bay. And my company doesn't do anything halfway, no siree. These new properties are going to be a *giant* boost to the local economy—not to mention what this is going to do for you, Bonnie. And for you too, Ben."

The man held Ben's eye just a moment too long.

And Ben knew. He *knew* it!

But he asked the question anyway.

"What's the name of your company, Mr. Birch?"

The man smiled broadly and looked Ben dead in the eyes.

"Glennley Properties, son. A *great* company!"

Ben narrowed his eyes, but he didn't blink or look away. *It wasn't so 'great,' what Glennley did for the area around the Shiloh Civil War Battlefield, with those rolling meadows turned into strip malls and fast food joints—that's what your 'great' company does best!*

Ben didn't say that out loud, but he thought it, and he felt like this man could see him thinking it.

But this guy was tough. He didn't blink either.

Ben said, "It's going to be really exciting to see how all this turns out, isn't it?"

The man kept smiling. "Yes, it is, son. Yes, it is."

"Well, it was good to meet you Mr. Lyman—oops, I mean, Mr. Birch!"

The man's smile wavered and his eyes widened. And then he blinked.

Ben turned and went to the kitchen and got himself that milk.

The conversation in the family room went on, but Ben tuned it out and carried the glass back up to his room. It was quiet up there, and he needed to think.

This was nasty stuff. They'd come to his mom with promises of real money, *big* money. Because they were after *him*.

It was like what Lyman had said to Jill that day in the library, telling her how her dad had bought all that stock in Glennley Group—to get her to stop trying to protect the school.

It hadn't worked on Jill, and it wasn't going to work on him.

This was just more evidence, proof that Glennley had to be stopped. They'd sent this Mr. Birch to tell lies to his mom, pretending she'd been picked over all the other real estate agents in Edgeport because she was so talented. And when she found out their real reason for choosing her, it was going to hurt her feelings. She'd deal with it, of course.

But it was still a rotten thing to do.

Ben realized his jaw was hurting from gritting his teeth so hard.

He relaxed and made himself take a long drink of milk. . . . Much better.

But if Lyman and the rest of the Glennley goon squad thought something like this was gonna slow *him* down, they were in for a big surprise.

CHAPTER 8

Snap Judgment

Eating Chinese with his mom wasn't fun at all.

"Isn't it *wonderful*, Ben? These people really know their business, and Jim is such a good guy, too—I'll be reporting to him directly. I can't wait to get started. It's like a dream come true!"

More like a nightmare, Ben thought. He had to keep smiling and nodding as he tried not to choke on his pork fried rice.

What these people were doing to his mom? It was so *wrong*!

In his room after supper he called Jill and told her the whole thing.

"Did you tell Robert yet?" she asked.

"No. I almost didn't tell you—but don't take that the wrong way. It's not like I was gonna back off from our work or anything so my mom would get all that money. I . . . I just don't want other people knowing about this. I feel so bad for her. That's all."

Jill was quiet. "My dad buys real estate at least a couple of times a year. And I know he never does *anything* without his lawyer. I think you need to talk to a good lawyer, the kind who specializes in real estate. I'll call you back."

The line clicked dead.

Ben stared at his phone. Her dad's lawyer? That was a terrible idea!

He punched redial, but it went right to Jill's message. He did that four more times before he tossed the phone on his bed, disgusted.

He leaned back in his desk chair and looked out the window, which ran up the slanted wall of his room. The sky was mostly clear, and some high-flying gulls looked gold, painted by the last beams of daylight. It was the kind of scene that usually made him feel good just to be alive. Not tonight.

I shouldn't have called her! No matter which way this spins, Mom gets hurt!

He pounced when his phone buzzed.

"I sure hope you didn't call your dad's—"

Jill cut him off. "What, my dad's lawyer? Do you think I'm that stupid, Benjamin? I called Amanda Burgess."

She was also a lawyer, and Ben liked her. They'd talked with her after finding that codicil, the addition to the captain's will. But she hadn't been able to help because she was already involved in the case.

"Of course, I didn't tell her anything," Jill went on, "but I did ask her to recommend a good real estate lawyer, someone we can trust *and* someone we can call right now, tonight. And I told her we can pay real fees, too. Got a pencil?"

"Um . . . yes," said Ben.

"His name is Harold Chamden, and Mrs. Burgess said she'd warn him, so he wouldn't think you were some kid pranking him." She read Ben the phone number.

Then she said, "So, the second I hang up, you call him. You want to know three simple things: one, can he look in public records and see exactly what properties Glennley has been buying during the past year; two, are the deals final; and three, is there any way to stop or delay any of them. And you can tell him we've got plenty of money to work with. These people try to mess with us, we mess with them."

Ben hesitated, then said, "Is this . . . I mean, can we . . . like, is this kind of thing even legal?"

"How should I know?" she said. "Ask your lawyer!"

And for the second time in ten minutes, Jill hung up on him.

CHAPTER 9

Ready, Aim, Spend!

Harold Chamden picked up the phone during the first ring and started talking a mile a minute.

"Hey! This is Benjamin, right? Just got an earful from Amanda—said you and your friend Jill are the real deal. Tell me what's up, and tell me everything, okay? No one else hears what you say to me, ever. Start at the start, and take it slow so I can take notes."

Ben didn't know where to begin. "Um, well . . . about three weeks ago . . . well, first, there was this old janitor . . . but really it's mostly about the Captain Oakes School . . . and . . ."

The lawyer helped him out. He began again, speaking more slowly.

"Look, Ben—may I call you Ben?"

"Sure."

"Good. So, Ben, think a second about what made you want to call me tonight, and tell me that part first."

"Well, my mom's a real estate agent. . . ."

"And a good one, I have to add," said the lawyer. "I've been involved in at least a dozen deals with her during the past ten years or so, and she's a real professional, straight up. And as I mentioned, whatever you say here is just between us."

"So," Ben resumed, "this man named Jim Birch has been talking to my mom, and he says he's making her the main broker for selling hundreds of new condominiums up and down the coast. I know she's good, but I also know for sure that this guy is making her this offer because he wants to stop *me*. From doing something."

Harold Chamden took a moment to think about that. "And can you tell me what he'd like to stop you from doing?"

"He wants to make me and my friends stop

trying to save the Oakes School from being torn down. And stopping the whole Tall Ships Ahoy! theme park. We're working to keep that from happening, and this man knows it. So he's pushing all this money at my mom to make me feel like I have to stop."

"And your mother doesn't know what you're doing about the school?"

"No, almost nobody knows. There are five of us—we're called Keepers. And also a guy at Edgeport Trust and Savings Bank, he knows too. And I think Mrs. Burgess has a pretty good idea what we're up to, but she's not allowed to talk to us about it. Because of ethics."

"Well, Ben, here's what I already know, just because you mentioned that one name, Jimmy Birch. Every real estate lawyer in Essex County knows about this operator, and what he's been trying to do for the Glennley Group. He's a greasy-sleazy-makes-me-queasy kind of lawyer. Started making offers on properties about eighteen months ago, came in with high bids every time."

"So . . . is Glennley really doing all the stuff this man told my mom about?"

"Not exactly. I'm on the Realty Ethics Board, and when the papers were filed on the first property Mr. Birch went after, we heard about it. They haven't really been buying properties. They've been buying *options* to buy—they pay a little bit now, to lock up the right to *actually* buy at a time in the future. They don't really *own* a thing, not yet. And after that first deal, our ethics board made sure that all the other sellers got good legal advice. Thanks to us, most of the sellers now have ways to get out of the Glennley options—

if someone else offered them more money, for instance."

Ben was pleased with himself—he was actually understanding what the lawyer was saying, and he liked what he heard. And he remembered that money was an important part of every war he'd ever read about, even the American Revolution. If the French hadn't supported the colonists with loans and donations, the war might have been lost. And now, Mr. Birch and the Glennley Group thought they could change the course of *this* war with a pile of money.

Well guess what, buddy? Ben thought. Two can play this game!

Using his most grown-up sounding voice, Ben said, "So, if you were the Glennley Group, Mr. Chamden, and all of Mr. Birch's real estate deals suddenly fell apart, would that make you feel like the Tall Ships Ahoy! project wasn't worth doing?"

"Not worth doing at all?" said the lawyer. "No . . . but it would certainly make the whole plan a lot less desirable, much less profitable. And the Glennley stockholders wouldn't like that one bit."

"About how much money has Glennley spent on these options so far?" Ben asked.

"Three or four million dollars. But the total value of all the properties is more like twenty million. Of course, then they plan to tear down the homes and the other structures they've optioned and put up new condominium buildings. So that twenty million is just the beginning of what they plan to invest."

"Yes, sir," Ben said, "but they have to buy all the land *first*, right? And that's about twenty million dollars?"

"Right."

"So . . . how much would someone need to have to take those options away from Glennley?"

The lawyer chuckled. "A lot, Ben. Probably about twenty-five, maybe thirty million dollars. And frankly, son, in this real estate market, no one's going to step up and start a bidding war with the Glennley Group. It's just not—"

"Mr. Chamden, if I can find the money, what would you charge to do all the legal stuff, all the paperwork and everything?"

"Just my normal billing fees, Ben, but that could add up to fifteen or twenty thousand dollars when all's said and done, and I really don't—"

"Sorry to be rude, Mr. Chamden, but I've got to

make some other phone calls now. But I'm going to call you tomorrow, okay? And be sure to charge me for your time just now, okay? Good-bye, and thanks a lot!"

"Good night, Ben."

The lawyer sounded like he was saying good night to a three-year-old who had just explained how he was going to fly to Mars on the back of a monkey.

Ben had to smile. Because if everything went the way he thought it would, Mr. Harold Chamden would be meeting at the bank tomorrow with Mr. Arthur Rydens, the man in charge of the giant trust fund. He only hoped someone would be there to take a picture of the lawyer's face!

And using the camera on his phone, Ben took a snapshot of his own face as he called Jill to give her the news from the financial battlefield, and then a second photo when he called Robert a few minutes later.

They were great pictures.

CHAPTER 10

Tip of the Spear

Ben and Jill and Robert were waiting at the front door of the school on Tuesday before Mrs. Hendon had even turned on all the lights in the office. She buzzed them in, and they headed straight for the long hallway, the one with the post that went *bong*.

Lyman knew that the three kids had permission slips for entering the school early, and every day for the past two weeks, his gray pickup truck had been parked at the loading dock by seven fifteen. But today Lyman was going to be late.

At precisely six minutes after seven o'clock,

Mrs. Keane's old Plymouth had stalled near the corner of Salem and Beecham Street, and there was quite a traffic snarl—the worst one Edgeport had seen in months, maybe years. Cars and trucks and school buses were backed up four or five blocks in both directions. And to the north, the traffic jam went well past Buckman Court. Which meant that while Lyman could drive his truck out of his driveway, he couldn't turn onto Salem Street in either direction.

They worked fast—Wally would certainly arrive any second. In her backpack, Jill had a brand-new ScanMaster 9000, a small, powerful device for detecting all kinds of radio signals—including the kind emitted by wireless video cameras. Before the Keepers showed any interest in a particular post in this hallway, they had to be certain no one was watching.

Jill made two passes along the hall, going from the art room to the south staircase, and then back again.

"Any signals?" Ben asked.

"Nope, just a weak blip when I passed the janitor's room. The hallway is clean."

"Great!" said Robert. He pulled out their new

camera and trotted to the fourth post from the art room wall. Beginning near the ceiling, he snapped more than a dozen photos, a full set with flash, and another set without.

The whole process of scanning and photographing took less than five minutes.

"Okay," Ben said. "Let's go up to the second floor now and study the walls over on the other side of the school."

Jill looked at him like he was crazy.

But Robert smiled and said, "Great idea, Pratt."

Then Jill got it too. "Oh—so Wally will find us there—let's go! And I'll keep the scanner on."

"Don't bother," Robert said. "We *want* them to see us messing around up on the second floor."

"No," Ben said, "we should scan everywhere we can. We should know about any cameras or microphones—even if we do want to be observed right now."

"Yeah . . . I guess," Robert conceded. "But we don't want to run down the batteries in that thing."

Ben saw Jill smile slightly at that. Robert still had trouble admitting it when he made a mistake. Which wasn't very often . . . and that was good.

They'd only been up in the north hallway on the second floor for about three minutes when they heard a door slam in the stairwell, then footsteps running up the stairs.

"Get ready—and don't forget to look guilty and worried!" Ben said.

They heard the footsteps reach the landing.

"Now!" whispered Ben, and when Wally pulled the door open and burst into the hall, they were all whispering gibberish to each other as they stuffed papers and tape measures and the camera into their backpacks.

Wally looked like he'd just finished a marathon for short, out-of-shape people—huffing and puffing, a little unsteady on his feet, with dark sweat stains on his green shirt.

He leaned against the wall, "Busy morning, children? Looks like it. Hope you're having fun. Find anything interesting you'd like to share?"

Jill looked at him, clutching her backpack to her chest. "I can share something, sir. You need a shower!"

Ben tugged on her sleeve. "C'mon, let's go!"

But Jill pulled away from him.

"And I also think you need to start looking for a new job, sir. Because you're probably going to get *fired* after you fail at this important assignment, sir. But getting *fired* is something you're used to, isn't it? Sir."

Ben watched Wally's face getting redder and redder as Jill kept talking. His small eyes narrowed to slits, and the short dark hair on his head bristled like fur on the shoulders of an angry dog.

Robert had already hurried away toward the south stairwell without a word, which had been their plan. They were all going to meet up in the library.

Ben hissed, "Jill, let's go! Come on—*now*!"

Jill kept her eyes locked with Wally's and said to Ben, "Let's go *this* way."

She walked straight toward Wally, and Ben had no choice but to follow. He double-stepped and managed to get around to Jill's left, so he'd be between her and Wally as they went into the north stairwell. The look on the guy's face was flat-out scary.

But Wally didn't say a word, didn't move a muscle as they went past him less than a foot away—Jill was right about that shower.

They started down the stairs, and when they reached the landing, the door above them opened and Wally came along behind.

Ben tried to hustle her along, but Jill took her time. She walked like she was taking a stroll on the beach. And then she started talking—loud enough so Wally could hear every word.

"You know what I love about this school, Ben? I love how *clean* it is. We have *terrific* janitors here, don't you think? I mean, they really know how to shove a broom and mop out a bathroom. And that new guy? Have you seen his technique? He's a true master, sort of a cross between a samurai and a rodeo clown. That man can do it all. I wouldn't be surprised if he makes it to the big leagues one day—he could work at a fish market . . . or a pet hospital, someplace that's *super* messy. Because this guy has All-Star Janitor written all over him."

Ben was relieved when they got to the library.

Ms. Shubert was working at the main desk, so Jill finally had to shut up.

"What's the *matter* with you?" he hissed.

She whispered right back, "It's called *strategy*, Benjamin. Because the things I learned about Mr. Wallace Robleton last night were very interesting. This guy has serious anger issues. And if we can get him to blow his top, he'll be out of here—gone!"

Ben was surprised at her answer—because it was exactly what he'd tried to do to Lyman yesterday morning before homeroom.

So . . . what? We're all turning into killers now . . . going straight for the throat?

They'd been walking toward the alcove along the east wall, and as they got close, Robert put a finger to his lips and held up a note aimed at Jill—one word: SCAN!

She nodded and reached a hand into her backpack. She tilted her head, listening—she was still wearing the tiny Bluetooth earpiece that was linked to the signal scanner.

After a moment she said, "All clear."

As they sat down, Ben said, "So, what exactly did you learn about Wally?"

Jill raised an eyebrow. "A *lot*. Unlike Lyman, he has no degrees beyond high school. But after living at home for a year or two, he joined the navy, and they tested him and found he had a good head for math and science. So he took a ton of classes and became a telecommunications expert—radio, radar, satellites, plus all kinds of computer skills. He's a very smart guy."

"But you said he has anger issues . . ."

"Right. Mostly, it seems like he can't stand stupid people. He was discharged from the navy after he tackled a superior officer who wouldn't let him do a project he thought was important."

"And then?" Robert prompted.

"He went back to his hometown of Charlottesville, Virginia, married a girl he'd known there, but got divorced after a year—same deal, anger issues. She had to take out a restraining order. No kids."

"How'd you find all this?" said Ben.

"Hometown newspapers, public records search, the usual ways. It's all out there, and the Internet never forgets. He's got a pretty unusual name. But I did have to spend about forty dollars to check for criminal history—I used our credit card."

"Criminal history? He has a record?"

"Arrests, but no convictions. He worked for Engleton Computing after the navy, and got fired for using company server space to host his own website to sell discount patio furniture. Charges were filed with the police, but then dropped. About a year later he was working at a place called Carleton Trucking Company, and he got fired after he used a company warehouse for a huge weekend party. He was charged with criminal trespass and destruction of private property. But after he paid about two thousand dollars for cleaning and repairs, the charges were dropped. And then at a company called East Shore Logistics, he got fired for using a company truck to haul loads of firewood from his dad's farmland in Virginia to a friend's garden center in Bethesda, Maryland. He was charged with illegal use of private property, but the charges were dropped. And he was fired. So, basically, what we have with Wally is a smart guy who's lucky not to be sitting in jail somewhere."

Robert said, "But with all that stuff in his past, how come he got hired by Glennley? It doesn't make sense."

"Not until you look at the yearbook of Lewellton Academy in Chicago, Illinois. Because young Wally was on the football team there, and he played center. And I'll give you three guesses to figure out who he was hiking the ball to."

"Really?" said Ben. "*Lyman* was the quarterback?"

"Yup, and he was pretty good, too. The team got to the state final of the private school league their senior year. But in the last three minutes of the game, Wally slugged a player on the other team and got sent to the locker room. And when the substitute center hiked the ball on a crucial play, he wobbled it, and Lyman fumbled, and the other team recovered. They lost the game and the title. But those two must have stayed friends over the years, because when Lyman needed help here, he called up his old teammate. Oh—and guess what Wally's nickname was in high school."

"Really?!" Robert exclaimed. "*Stumpy*?"

Jill smiled and shook her head. "Nope, but close. They called him the Fireplug."

Robert grinned. "Nice—that's even better!"

The three of them sat quietly. It was a lot of new information to process.

Ben had trouble imagining Lyman as a high school kid—a tall, skinny quarterback, calling the plays in a big game. And losing at the last minute after his friend got tossed from the game? It made the guy seem a little more human. Ben caught himself feeling kind of sorry for Lyman—really, for both of them. But he remembered the mission at hand and flipped that feeling on its head. Because this information also made Lyman and Wally more vulnerable, which was what intelligence gathering was all about . . . right? Going for the throat. . . .

I don't think I'd be a very good soldier . . . but I have to be! I have to!

"Speaking of the devil . . . ," Robert muttered, nodding toward the door.

Ben turned. It was Wally, still glaring at them, still sweaty.

Again, a kind of pity welled up in Ben's heart. But he fought it and forced himself to see an enemy standing there, made himself pretend that the long handle of Wally's dust mop was a rifle—with fixed bayonet.

Because there was no room for softness now, no room for anything but tough, sharp, straight-ahead fighting, with no holds barred. He was right at the tip of the spear in this battle, so he had to think and act that way every second . . . right?

Right!

That's what Ben's mind told him.

His heart wasn't quite so certain.

CHAPTER 11

Twenty-First Century Warriors

It was 7:55, and just as the entry bell clanged, Robert said, "I've got something for you guys, and for me, too."

He glanced toward the doorway—Wally wasn't in sight. Reaching into his backpack, he pulled out three iPads.

"I know this seems kind of over the top, but I got the cheapest ones available with the least amount of storage. But I did pay a little extra to get cellular connectivity along with the Wi-Fi. Plus, I bought a really fast portable Wi-Fi hotspot device with about six hours of battery life, so we can set up our own private network if we need one. And when you two were taking your sweet time getting back here, I opened a Bluetooth connection to the new camera and uploaded all the pictures I took of the post in the hallway, and all the other photos we've got too. So we can each study them. And we all have access to a secure cloud storage space too—touch the app called Notes, and you'll see some instructions and the password for that. These things also take pretty good pictures and movies. And you can text, and there's also video conferencing if we need it. I mean, I know these aren't *absolutely* necessary, but . . . portable communication matters a lot right now, don't you think?"

Jill held out her hand right away, and Robert passed her the one with the blue cover. "Great!" she said. "But, of course, when this work's done, we'll sell them and put the money back into the trust account."

"Oh, absolutely!" said Robert.

Ben had to hide a smile. Jill was getting very comfy with the idea of buying whatever they needed. She hadn't batted an eye last night about spending twenty-two million dollars to shut down the Glennley real estate attack, and neither had Robert. That whole plan was moving ahead, and the lawyer was meeting Tom Benton and Mrs. Keane at the bank this morning to sign some papers.

Robert handed him the iPad with the gray cover. He flipped it open, and the screen lit up. There was a keypad labeled ENTER PASSCODE.

"What's the code?" he asked.

"Four letters," Robert whispered, "*k, p, r, s*."

"Nice!"

Jill frowned as she tapped in the code. "But . . . what do I tell my mom? 'Cause we can't leave these at school, and she's gonna find this thing at home, I know she will."

Ben had wondered the exact same thing, and he got it. "Just tell her the truth—it's on loan to you as part of a grant from Edgeport Bank and Trust . . . in support of our Oakes School history project. And if she's got a problem with that, she can call Mr. Rydens at the bank!"

Robert grinned. "Good one, Pratt!"

Jill smiled too. "And really, we could tell that to anybody here at school who asks where we got them—but . . . is having this at school even allowed?"

"Are you kidding?" said Robert. "You need to read the town newspaper more often. The school department's gonna *give* one of these to every single kid in fourth through twelfth grade next year—spending Glennley's money, I bet. There are rules about when and how they can be used, but it's already okay for a kid to have an iPad at any school in town."

Ben had the photo app open, checking out the pictures of the post—the images were so clear, and he knew how to make the screen do what he wanted it to. One afternoon while his mom had shopped at the Burlington Mall, he'd spent almost two hours at a store messing with the display models. But having one of his own to use? It was great, except . . .

"Hey, guys?" he said. "We're gonna have to watch our time with these things."

"Right!" Jill said. "This is a tool, not a toy—so, no goofing off, no downloading games or music. Okay?"

They all nodded, but their eyes never left the screens.

Then Robert said, "Except Pratt has permission

to download a beginner's sailing simulator to get ready for our race on Saturday—he's gonna need all the help he can get!"

"Ha-ha, very funny. You need to put up your own website, Gerritt—How to Flip an Optimist onto Your Head in One Easy Lesson!"

Ten minutes later the clang of the homeroom warning bell pulled them back to reality. Ben was first on his feet.

"Well, I have zero ideas about what a brass post that looks exactly like wood has to do with us finding a safeguard—and I've studied every single picture we've got. You guys see anything?"

"Um, I was looking at the iPad instruction manual in the books app," Jill said. "But I'll check out the photos during homeroom."

"Better not," Robert said. "You pull that out, and there'll be a crowd, and then you'll have to start explaining . . . which is just my opinion, of course," he added quickly. "I'm sure you'll handle whatever comes up."

Ben said, "See you guys later. And thanks, Gerritt—this was a good move."

He could have walked the short way to homeroom, but Ben went out of the library and turned left, walked past the office, and then went along the hall by the janitor's room—the same route he'd taken yesterday when he was whacking each post.

He didn't see Lyman or Wally, so he took a good look at the fourth post from the art room. Nothing unusual at all.

Walking on, he counted his steps to the door of the art room—thirteen . . . so at around three feet per stride, that meant the posts were about twelve feet apart—seemed right.

He tried to visualize what was on the other side of that hallway wall, because there wasn't a classroom there between the janitor's room and the art room. And he knew that the janitor's room didn't extend that far along the hallway. Even though the art room sort of made an L shape, it certainly didn't extend back twenty or thirty feet. . . .

And then it hit him. He felt stupid not to have realized it sooner. Because in the art room, in the back corner of the L, there was a door.

He'd seen it standing open plenty of times,

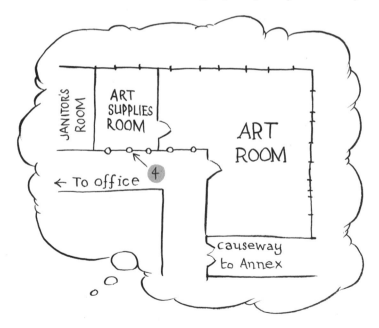

seen the gray metal racks with the wide rolls of colored paper, seen the stacks of easels, seen all the shelves loaded with twenty different kinds of paper, large plastic canisters of tempera paint, bags of clay, bottles of glue—lots and lots of shelves that ran back toward the janitor's room wall.

And then another thought! It was so simple it was almost stupid—walls have *two* sides, and so do thick posts! So it was entirely possible that the *other* side of post number four would be visible on the *other* side of the hallway wall!

Walking into homeroom, Ben's heart was thumping out a double-time march. Some way, somehow, during the next fifty-seven minutes, he was going to visit the art supplies room.

CHAPTER 12

Stowaway

"Have you seen Ben?"

Jill was with Robert on the front steps after school.

He shook his head. "Not since sixth period. All he said was that he wasn't going to meet us in the library after school. Did he text you or anything?"

"Nope. Maybe he just went home—he could be there by now. You want to give him a call?"

"Not me," said Robert. Then, with half a smile, he said, "Call him yourself, if you're so worried."

"I'm not *worried*, Gerritt. Everybody keeps saying there's not a second to waste, so I was thinking we'd try to do something this afternoon, make some progress. That's all."

Robert shrugged. "He probably ran off to the marina to sneak a practice session with his new boat—so he doesn't get completely schooled on Saturday."

Jill rolled her eyes. "You two and your toy boats—it makes me tired. I'm going home."

"Yeah, me too." Robert jerked his thumb toward the front door. "Stumpy needs a break!"

Jill glanced over her shoulder. There in the window of the right hand door she saw Wally, standing watch. She smiled and waved at him, then stuck out her tongue. And immediately wished she hadn't—not exactly a mature thing to do.

She went straight down the steps, and when she reached the harbor walk, headed south toward home. She looked over her shoulder to be sure Robert couldn't see her, then pulled out her phone and called Ben.

It went right to message.

Ben felt his phone vibrate and quickly pushed the reject button. It seemed so loud!

He was sitting alone in the dark, living with

the results of decisions and discoveries he had made during the day.

Most importantly, he'd decided not to tell Jill or Robert his ideas about the art supplies room. They were both so much smarter than he was—or at least it felt that way. He wanted to check it out on his own before he said anything. And if there was nothing, then he wouldn't have to mention it at all.

There was also the risk factor. What he had in mind could backfire, and if there was trouble, why have it knock Jill or Robert out of action? Better if they didn't even know. They wouldn't have to lie. Or get kicked out of school before the last week. Or have another scary meeting with the principal.

As he ticked through the possible dangers, twice Ben caught himself thinking mostly about protecting Jill—and he quickly added *and Robert too*.

He'd checked the supplies room door during homeroom—locked. He had Mr. Keane's keys in his book bag, but if he tried to mess with the door, people would notice.

So he'd approached the problem in stages,

and he started by waiting until homeroom ended and first period art began.

The class was working on decorations for the final chorus concert, and since it was an all-American theme, red, white, and blue tempera paints were in high demand. Fifteen minutes into the class, the red paint pot was half empty, and Ben casually took it and dumped what was left down the drain of the big sink.

Then he'd gone to Ms. Wilton and said, "We need more red paint—should I mix some up?"

"That'd be great, Ben. There's a container on the shelf over the sink."

"Nope, no red—I already checked." Which he had.

Ms. Wilton did just what Ben had hoped she would. She pulled open the file drawer of her desk, found a key, and handed it to him. "Go check the supplies room for me, will you? The tempera is on the wooden shelves near the back. Better bring two. Thanks!"

So that was Ben's first tour of the room, and even though it had lasted less than two minutes, he accomplished three important things.

The first was simply to confirm what he'd

already guessed: Some of the thick wooden hallway posts *did* extend through the wall into the supplies room—three of them, including the one that sounded like a gong if you whacked it. With a baseball.

The second important thing he did was to take a good close-up picture of the supply room key with his cell phone—a photo he'd be able to compare with the keys on Mr. Keane's key ring.

The third thing was actually something he *didn't* do. As he walked out of the supplies room with two big plastic jars of red tempera powder, he *didn't* relock the door.

He'd hoped there would be a way to slip back inside during class, but it hadn't worked out. Most of the concert decorations were made of large pieces of cardboard, and they were spread out on every table plus all over the floor, including the area near the supplies room.

First period was ending, and just when Ben had started feeling like he would have to ask Jill and Robert for help with this, Ms. Wilton waved a paper in the air and made an announcement.

"Listen, everyone—quiet down! This is a sign-up sheet. I need volunteers to help with decorations in the auditorium after school, so if you can do that, meet here at ten of three, all right? It'll take half an hour at the most. *And* there'll be refreshments!"

A group of kids quickly volunteered, but Ben wasn't among them. He saw a glimmer of a plan, and by the end of the school day, he'd worked it out . . . except for a few wrinkles.

When he saw Jill and Robert during the rest of Tuesday, he felt bad about not bringing them in on this . . . but not bad enough to risk them watching his idea fizzle. Besides, he knew Robert would try to take over the whole operation—that was what he'd done with the Underground Railroad business last week.

As sixth period had ended, he was ready to put his plan into motion—and to deal with the consequences.

Wally was standing watch in the hall outside the gym, but Ben had been ready for that. He was the first kid through the doors of the gym and just took off running. He got a quick twenty-yard head start on Wally, and when the hallway filled with kids, the stocky janitor with his wide dust mop fell farther behind.

And Ben had made sure Wally saw him as he

took a left at the first hallway intersection by the music room. But Wally had *not* seen him instantly duck into the auditorium, run all the way across the back of the stage, out the far door, and then turn right. Almost running, he'd sped through the causeway from the Annex and into the old building—unseen by Wally or Lyman.

And at that point, he'd ducked into the boys' restroom nearest the art room—which was also pretty close the janitor's workshop. He went into the fourth stall, the one at the end by the wall, but he didn't close the door. Instead, he got both feet up on the seat of the toilet, a trick he'd seen in a movie. Unless someone walked right down in front of the last stall, it looked unoccupied, with the door hanging open and no feet showing below the metal dividers.

The waiting had been the worst part—almost ten minutes of squatting above that toilet. His feet and legs had ached at first, and then they'd started to go numb.

Ben could tell the buses had left, and the school got a lot quieter. He could hear Ms. Wilton, thirty feet away at the art room doorway.

"Careful, Luke—don't try to carry everything!

Jana, grab that bag—no the one with the staplers and the string. And don't touch the panels by the windows—they're not dry yet! Good, let's go."

When that noise had faded into the distance, he was ready to climb down—but suddenly he heard Wally in the hall just outside the washroom door. Actually, it was Lyman he heard first, talking through the two-way speaker clipped to Wally's shirt.

"Seen unit three yet?"

Ben heard the washroom door open, heard Wally shuffle inside.

"No. Securing first floor south."

Wally's voice was loud, so close.

Then Lyman's reply crackled with urgency.

"Get to the east door—I've spotted units one and two!"

Ben held his breath and didn't exhale until the boys' room door had hissed shut. He heard Wally's footsteps hurrying toward the office.

His legs were stiff as he climbed down off the toilet seat, and then came the pins and needles. Ignoring that as best he could, he pulled the door open a crack: no one in sight toward the office . . . and no one but two fourth graders coming from the other direction.

The next fifteen seconds ticked past perfectly. He slipped out of the boy's room, took ten quick strides to the art room door—which wasn't locked. He stepped inside without being seen, hurried to the back of the L, and walked into the supplies room—also unlocked. And then he promptly locked the door from the inside.

He hadn't turned on the overhead lights in the room, which is why he was sitting in the dark when his cell phone buzzed.

He pulled the phone out—a call from Jill. No message.

Ben remembered just last week, how the two of them had stood side by side in the darkness underneath the south staircase, with Lyman's dog sniffing and scratching inches away on the other side of a wall. And Jill had grabbed his hand, and then held on. For five minutes.

Ben felt a sudden twinge and wished she were with him now . . . not holding hands, he quickly told himself. Just helping out. In the dark.

Well, almost dark—a little light filtered in under the door.

He lit up his phone to check the time: already

three fifteen, so the decorations party would be over any minute. Then he'd be able to do some real snooping. He had a fresh battery in his flashlight, so the moment the coast was clear, he was good to go.

He heard footsteps in the hall, and then the art room door opened—Ms. Wilton was back to lock up. . . .

"The little punks are gone."

Ben almost dropped his phone—Wally's voice.

"Language!" barked Lyman, and Ben could hear him moving around the art room, emptying trash barrels.

"Right," came Wally's sarcastic reply over the two-way radio. "Units one and two have left—is that better?"

"Nothing on unit three?"

Lyman made little grunts as he shoved the dust mop around.

"I think he left too."

"Well, look sharp, and start sweeping the third floor."

"Aye, aye, captain."

"And cut the funny stuff!" Lyman snapped.

Wally didn't reply.

The dust mop thumped against the supplies room door, and then Lyman jiggled the knob. Ben was ready to drop to the floor and roll for cover, but the door stayed shut.

And then Ms. Wilton's voice.

"Hi Jerry—sorry for the extra mess in here. It'll all be over soon, right? Any day now, and you can stop bothering to clean up at all, what with the demolition coming. Anyhow, thanks."

"You're welcome," Lyman said. Ben could hear the wheels of the trash cart moving away—so Lyman was gone. A minute later, the art room lights clicked off, the hallway door closed, and he heard Ms. Wilton's brisk footsteps as she walked along the causeway toward the faculty parking lot.

Ben pulled out his phone again. He had to send a text.

Hi mom. At school late—history project. Probly home after 5. Don't worry, call if you need me. Love, ben

The school around him got quieter and quieter—not quite as still as it was at three in the morning, but close.

For a moment Ben felt like he was hiding deep inside the hold of an old ship, down below the waterline—a stowaway, looking for adventure on the high seas.

Except that wasn't it at all. He was *not* a stowaway. He was on a secret mission, and Captain Oakes himself had given him very specific orders.

This was war, and there was work to do.

CHAPTER 13

Deep Cover

Ben used his flashlight to take a good look around the art supplies room, making a mental map as he did.

Except for the area on either side of the door, all the walls were lined with shelving units, some made of wood and others of metal. And the center of the room was also filled with metal shelving. Not surprisingly, most of the shelves in the room were empty. All kinds of supplies and equipment from Oakes School had been moved to other schools in the district and to storage locations, a steady stream for the past month or so, getting ready for the big teardown.

The entry door was on the west wall, which backed up against the art room. The east wall, about twenty-five feet away, backed up onto the janitor's workroom—and Ben reminded himself that silence was critical.

The south wall of the room was brick, the outer wall of the school. It had four wide windows just like the ones in the art room, except these windows had been nailed shut, and the glass had been painted over with the same thick brown paint that covered the walls.

The north wall was the important one, the one that backed up against the hallway. Three of the hallway posts—the foot-hooks—were right there, just above the wooden shelves.

Ben had already figured out that the middle post was the fourth one from the corner out in the hall, the one that sounded like brass. Looking carefully with his light, the part of the center post visible above the wooden shelf unit looked no different from the other two posts.

Immediately, Ben saw something different about the shelves that ran along the north wall, the shelves that covered the lower six feet of each post. Unlike the shelves elsewhere in the room, these wooden shelves were old—very similar to the heavy oak bookcases that lined the outer walls of the library, bookcases that dated back to the 1780s. The long wall of shelving was divided up into five sections—four wide ones, and one narrow one.

He felt like he was getting to know John Vining, the ship's carpenter who had done the actual work of concealing the captain's safeguards. There was no real reason to have one narrow shelf unit with wider ones on either side. John Vining had put the thinner one there on purpose, right in front of that *particular* post!

Ben began clearing the center shelf unit. It held mostly drawing and construction paper, and he stacked the packages gently on the metal shelves behind him. The unit was about eighteen inches wide, and about that deep as well, and when it was cleared, he got his light up close to the back of the unit. There was nothing much to see. All the joints back there looked tight, and when he tapped the back of the unit gently, it sounded solid, with no give at all.

But when he focused the bright beam on the outer edges of the unit, Ben smiled. There were face boards along the top and bottom of the shelf units running from wall to wall, boards that *should* have run without a break from the west wall to the east wall. But they didn't. There were two joints in the boards, top and bottom, one on each side of the center shelves. It meant that the narrow unit in the center was a completely separate object, and *that* meant that it could *move*!

Digging into his book bag, Ben found his stainless-steel ruler. He worked the thin edge of it into the crack between the center unit and the shelves on the left. Using it like a putty knife, he gently removed dust and dirt, dried paint, and hardened varnish. When the left-hand crack was clear, he did the same thing on the right-hand side.

The top! he thought, and using the front of the shelves like a ladder, he stepped up twice, and reaching back, he cleared the crack where the wall and the wooden post met the wood of the shelf unit. The top of the shelf was covered with thick dust and grime, but the seams were easy to clear out. Then, on both the right and left of the top of the unit, he cleaned out the cracks running from the wall out toward the front of the shelves.

He climbed down, got to his hands and knees, and began to work on the bottom of the unit where it met the floor. This was much harder, and he found himself using the ruler more like a saw than a putty knife. It was the old floor varnish that made it so tough, and it was especially difficult because he had to move so slowly, working as quietly as possible.

When he finished, he was panting, and sweat from his forehead dripped down onto the floorboards.

His hands were filthy. But this was a supplies room . . . yes! A big roll of brown paper towels. He tore off a length, wiped his face to get it damp, and then scrubbed most of the dirt off his hands and arms.

And now the dangerous part. He felt sure that this narrow shelf unit was supposed to move, to pull straight out, away from the wall. And from the front of that post.

First, Ben made himself stand still. He had to get his breathing back to normal and stop his heart from beating so fast.

When he felt calm enough, he walked carefully to the east wall, the one facing the janitor's workroom. He slipped into a space between two metal shelf units and laid his right ear flat against the painted plaster wall. He held his breath and listened. And listened. And listened.

Nothing—no voices, no sounds at all except a slight hum, sort of the kind a refrigerator makes.

Moving back to the narrow shelf unit, he laid his flashlight on the floor, braced his arms against the front of the top edge, and then flexed his legs upward as gently as he could . . . and it moved! Not much, but enough so he could tell that it wasn't nailed or screwed to the larger units on either side.

Encouraged, he pushed upward with a little more force, and again, there was give, and a pretty loud sound, sort of like a stick scratching on the sidewalk.

He froze, listening . . . listening. . . . Nothing.

Letting go of the top of the unit, he hooked the fingers of both hands under the front lip of the center shelf, which was about waist high.

Ben leaned back—didn't really pull, just leaned back. With only a slight scratching sound, and almost as smoothly as opening the drawer of a file cabinet, the whole narrow shelf unit rolled toward him—the ship's carpenter must have devised some sort of wheels under the shelf! Astonished, he kept pulling, and it came forward until it stood completely free of the shelf units on either side, a full twelve inches beyond their fronts.

His mouth felt completely dry. This was like a scene from a horror movie—the haunted mansion where someone touches something and a secret doorway glides open!

He grabbed his flashlight, stepping to his right

so he could aim the beam back into the space where the shelves had been. He needed to see the lower portion of the post, the hidden part.

That post was *not* made of brass—he saw that right away.

But set within the oak, completely surrounded by the dark wood, there was a panel that lay flush with the chiseled surface. And letting the small circle of light play across its surface, he knew that the panel was made of brass. Definitely.

The panel was about two feet high, and, at its widest, almost a foot wide. And staring at it, Ben shivered—he couldn't help it.

The panel was shaped like a coffin.

CHAPTER 14

Inside

While the coffin-shaped panel didn't look much like brass, Ben had been in enough salvage yards and antique shops to know that dark brownish color—it looked like the metal binding around the edges of old sea chests, or like heavy deck cleats that had seen too much weather and too little polishing.

Stepping closer, Ben tapped the panel lightly with the side of his thumb—it made a faint *bong*, the same tone he'd heard when he had struck the other side of the post out in the hallway. Definitely brass.

He made himself take a deep breath, slow

down. He had to be careful, methodical. First, he got out his phone and used the camera to take pictures, a lot of them. He even remembered to take a shot holding his ruler up against the post to establish the scale. He wished he had that new camera Robert had used this morning, but really all he needed to do was document the discovery, and for that his phone worked just fine.

He zoomed in as close as the tiny lens would let him and took a series of shots of the outer edge of the panel. There was some kind of black goo smeared all the way around the rim.

Ben leaned in close and sniffed—it smelled familiar . . . like pinecones. And then he knew! It was pine pitch, which was used by early shipbuilders for waterproofing. John Vining had used the sticky stuff to seal this container!

Up at the top corner of the coffin shape, Ben saw two pieces of metal wire, maybe copper, and the ends had been twisted into a loop. Moving his flashlight beam closer, he traced the two strands of wire right down into the pitch—they were actually buried in the stuff. Almost instinctively, Ben hooked his right index finger into the wire loop and pulled. There was a quick hissing sound, and Ben froze—the hair on his arms stood up.

But instantly he realized what had happened. It was like he'd just twisted the cap off a bottle of juice—this container had been vacuum sealed.

He kept pulling on the wire, and it tracked right around the edge of the brass panel, breaking the seam of pitch. Little bits of it popped loose and fell to the floor. And when the whole length of wire came free, so did the panel, leaning suddenly outward!

Almost in a panic, Ben slapped his left palm onto the panel to hold it in place, and not just to keep it from falling and making a huge noise. No, this was fear, and he pressed on the brass panel with all his strength.

Because what if this thing really was . . . a coffin? And there was something dead in there. He knew that people sometimes made tiny coffins for babies . . . he couldn't deal with *that*. Or . . . what if Captain Oakes had left one of his *hands* in there, cut off and holding some new message? This thing could contain almost anything—even a whole human head!

It was odd, but his little phone camera came to the rescue—it gave him a way to get some distance, to be one step removed from the scene in front of him. Still holding the panel in place, he dropped the freed wire, got out his cell phone, and clicked on the movie function. Holding his flashlight in his mouth, he aimed, pressed record, and the small LED light came on. Then, keeping his eyes *only* on that tiny screen, he moved his left hand up to the top of the brass panel, got a good grip on it, and slowly lowered it to the floor—it was heavy.

Despite the thrill of actually finding the next big clue, Ben felt a little disappointed. No mummi-

fied head stared out at him, no petrified hand with ruby rings on its skeleton fingers reached for his throat.

There was nothing inside the little brass coffin but a very ordinary looking parcel, as if Captain Oakes had bundled up a shirt or two and wrapped them in coarse sailcloth to send to the laundry. The package lay at an angle, propped up in the lower half of the coffin.

Ben turned off the camera and put the phone back in his pocket. He picked up the parcel. It wasn't even that heavy . . . but it certainly wasn't just shirts. He could feel something with sharp angles inside—maybe wood or metal. Looking at it up close, it was clear that someone had taken a great deal of care with the packing. The outer edges of the thick canvas were sewn together tightly, and where the wrapping overlapped, there

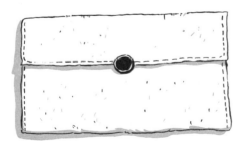

was a large blob of red sealing wax.

As carefully as possible, he slid the parcel into his book bag. The largest pocket was just deep enough, and he zipped it shut and set the bag against the wall by the door to the art room.

There was a sudden loud thump—he felt it through the floorboards. Then came a low rumble of voices, two men talking—Wally and Lyman. They were in the janitor's room, just the other side of the east wall, not twenty feet away. He couldn't make out any of their words.

Quickly and silently, Ben began to cover his tracks. He began by picking up the long copper wire. He bent it into a small coil and set it in the empty coffin space within the post. Using two sheets of poster board for a dustpan and brush, he swept up all the bits of scattered pitch he could see and dumped them in on top of the folded wire.

The brass lid of the coffin was a problem— without the pitch, it wouldn't remain where it had been—but he couldn't leave it resting on the floor behind the shelf, or it would keep the narrow shelf unit from rolling all the way back into place.

The wire!

Ben used his flashlight and looked on the other shelves until he found just what he needed—some metal pushpins.

He stuck two pins deep into the left side of the post with about a foot between them, and then pushed two matching pins deep into the wood on the right side of the post.

After straightening the wire, he wound one end of it around the push pin on the upper right. Lifting the brass lid and holding it in place, he stretched the wire across toward the bottom push

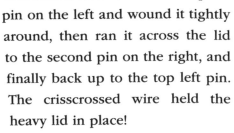

pin on the left and wound it tightly around, then ran it across the lid to the second pin on the right, and finally back up to the top left pin. The crisscrossed wire held the heavy lid in place!

He could still hear muffled talking from next door, and the safest thing would have been to sit still and wait for the enemy to move out. But he was too wound up to do that . . . and he felt sure he could work quietly. And really, all he had to do was slide the narrow shelf unit back into its slot.

He swept the floor behind it once more, making sure no little bits of pitch were in the way. Then, getting into position, he pushed the shelf unit toward the wall—very gently. Like a canoe gliding on a pond, the shelves rolled slowly across the floor, slipped almost noiselessly between the neighboring units, and settled into place.

Ben quickly restacked all the paper onto the shelves, exactly as they'd been before. Looking at the seams he had cleared out with his ruler, he gathered up some dust and grit in one hand, then spit in it and mixed up a grimy paste, which he then pushed into the open cracks with his thumb—gross but effective. He used the paper towel from earlier to clean his hands, and then wiped each of the seams before making a final inspection with his flashlight. It would have taken a Sherlock Holmes to discover what he'd been doing in here!

The tone of the voices in the next room changed it sounded like an argument. Again Ben pressed an ear against the east wall, but still couldn't make out what was being said in the janitor's room.

He remembered a trick he'd read about, and decided to give it a try. Taking out his phone, he found the voice memo app—it was just a simple recording application, and it used the small microphone on the bottom of the phone. Ben tapped the record button, then pressed the microphone against the wall and held it very still. Later at home, he could transfer the recording to his computer and make it much louder, maybe hear the voices more clearly, pick up some useful information.

I'm pretty good at this spy stuff! he said to himself.

Here he was, not fifteen feet from these guys, recording them, and they had no—

The sound was huge, like someone dropping a metal tray right behind him—a heavy tray that went *bong*! The coffin lid!

Ben sucked in a quick breath. . . .

It was immediately quiet, but then he knew a horrible truth . . . it was *too* quiet. The arguing in the janitor's room had stopped.

Seconds later he heard jangling keys.

Lyman and Wally were at the art room door.

CHAPTER 15

Standoff

Ben panicked, fought it back, then panicked again. A wave of heat rushed to his face. His hands shook as he grabbed his backpack and yanked it on, his mouth burning with the sharp coppery taste of raw fear.

Footsteps, more jangling keys, and the two of them, Lyman and Wally, were right on the other side of the door!

He scanned the room, the tiny flashlight beam jumping madly from wall to ceiling to floor, as if to spot some magic exit. If he'd had the strength, he'd have heaved a huge roll of craft paper through a window and leaped to freedom through the splintered sash.

There was no way out.

They would find the right key any second now.

They would walk in and flip on the lights.

There was no way out . . . except right through that door.

That door.

Those two men.

That door.

A sudden calm flowed across him like a curtain of mist.

Ben knew this feeling.

It was like the final leg of a race out on the bay, with two feet of chop and a hard crosswind. The hull bucks, the spray slashes, the sail snaps taut, there are three gallons to bail before taking the turn, and the red buoy is dead ahead. And in the middle of it comes a sharpness, a burst of clarity. It's all instinct, every twitch of the tiller, every shift of weight, every dip and duck and dodge, and in moments the buoy arrives—and then it's behind.

With no hesitation, Ben got a fresh grip on his cell phone, checked the settings, took four strong steps to the door, turned the knob, and pushed it open, blinking in the bright light.

The two men jumped backward, stunned for a second, and Ben took a quick step forward into the art room. And he also pushed the button that started the video recorder on his phone.

Lyman's face broke into a wide smile.

"Well, well, well—look what we have here, Wally. It's a *sneaky* little boy, caught after school . . . with his backpack full of stolen art supplies!"

"I didn't steal anything!"

"Wally and I *both* saw you, just now—you were pulling all sorts of stuff out of your bag, only a few moments after we heard a noise and came running. *You* are in very serious trouble, young man, very serious trouble indeed!"

Lyman turned to Wally who stood with a dull grin on his wide face. "I'll keep track of our little thief here while you run and fetch the principal— and maybe the principal should put in a call to the police."

"It's . . . it's your word against mine!" Ben spluttered.

"Exactly," said Lyman, his voice suddenly harsh. "Two witnesses against one—who do *you* think the principal is going to believe?"

As Ben struggled to reply, his phone buzzed.

He almost dropped it as he rushed to push talk—
barely spotting the tiny name on the screen.

"Jill! I'm in the art room with Wally and
Lyman, and they're gonna say I was stealing and
turn me in!"

Silence. Lyman kept smiling.

"You there? Jill?"

"I'm here. Put me on speaker, Benjamin."

Ben pushed the correct button and held on to
his phone with both hands, like it was the end of
a lifeline.

"Mr. Lyman, Mr. Robleton? Can you hear me?"

Lyman quickly tapped Wally and shook his
head, putting a finger to his lips.

Ben said, "They hear you, but they're not
going to say anything!"

"That works fine for me," she said. "Mr. Lyman,
if you and Mr. Robleton don't step aside and let
Ben walk out of there right now, this is what
happens. First, I call our attorney, and that is not
a bluff—we have a very good one on retainer.
The lawyer and I will prepare a press release with
factual information about who the two of you
are, who you both work for, what kind of work
you do, and we will have full details—all sorts of

information about your professional and personal histories, including the problems that your angry little friend—the one known as the Fireplug—has had with the law over the past fifteen years or so, issues that you both probably hid from the school superintendent in order for Wally to be allowed to even set foot inside a public school."

Wally's eyes narrowed, his face turning bright red. Ben nearly took a step backward, but held his ground. Jill sounded great, but Ben could tell she was scared too, and that she was having trouble finding the next thing to say. She kept talking.

"What the superintendent of schools has done will be exposed, how she hired two outside agents—without the knowledge of Principal Telmer—and how you two are being paid by both the town of Edgeport and the Glennley Group. We will also release our time-stamped photos of the Underground Railroad hideout, proving that *we* discovered that important historical place *first* . . . and how the discovery was stolen by Glennley and then used for their own selfish purposes. This press release, along with photos and video and all sorts of other information that you really cannot even *imagine*, Mr. Lyman, will

be e-mailed to all the major media outlets inside of one hour . . . and it will be big news by six o'clock tonight, guaranteed. Is this what you want, Mr. Lyman? Is this what you think your bosses want? And the reason I'm talking to you, Mr. Lyman, is because we all know that *you* are the quarterback here, right? And Ben, if that little Fireplug takes a swing at you, yell, and I'll hang up and dial 911—which will solve this problem in another way."

Wally raised his arm and tried to swat at Ben's phone, but Lyman stepped in front of him. The tall man's face was twisted with anger.

Ben said, "Lyman's thinking about it, Jill."

"Good," she said. "He should be. He should think very carefully. Because I have a sound recording of all of this. Can you snap a photo of the two of them there, Ben?"

"I already did!"

Ben kept his side of the phone turned so neither man could see it—this didn't seem like a good moment to reveal that he had a video of this whole thing.

"Great," Jill said. "So now let's state for the record that the time is exactly 3:47 p.m. on

Tuesday, June second, just in case either of those men even *touches* you, Benjamin. Because the laws about child endangerment in Massachusetts are very strict. In fact, Ben, I think it's perfectly safe for you to just step around Mr. Jerroald F. Lyman and Mr. Wallace V. Robleton, and walk right out of the Captain Duncan Oakes School. Ready?"

"Ready," Ben said.

He took a step toward the windows, and Wally lunged left, as if he intended to tackle him. Again, Lyman held him back, this time actually grabbing him with both arms.

Ben kept walking.

"I'm walking around them, and Lyman's holding Wally . . . and now I'm out in the hall!"

Jill yelled, *"Run!"*

Which was unnecessary.

Ben was already halfway down the causeway.

In four seconds he burst out the side door into the sunshine, and he didn't stop running till he reached his own back door on Walnut Street.

CHAPTER 16

Emergency Meeting

"This *isn't* the first time, Benjamin—why don't you just go ahead and do *everything* completely on your own from now on?"

Ben decided that "hissing" was too nice a word to describe the tone of Jill's voice. It sounded more the way a garbage disposal growls . . . or maybe the sound his front teeth would make if they were dragged along a sidewalk.

It was about seven thirty Tuesday night, and they were having an emergency Keepers meeting in his attic bedroom—he'd told his mom it was about their special project, which certainly was not a lie.

Ben sat there, his eyes cast down. He didn't argue, didn't offer any defense. Because then he'd have to admit how she and Robert made him feel nearly all the time—outsmarted. And out-clevered . . . out-everythinged. He thought he could have come right out and said that—if it were only to *her*.

But saying that with Robert right there? Wasn't gonna happen.

He had to say something . . . but he'd waited too long.

Jill added, "It's just so . . . so *immature*!"

Ben said, "Yeah, I know—sorry."

Robert said, "How about we lighten up, okay? I mean, the guy did get some *results*! So let's not forget about that. . . ."

Jill gave Robert the kind of look that's reserved for traitors. Or convicted kitten killers.

"So now it's all about *results,* is that it? Well, let's not forget that I had to tell our enemies a bunch of *our* secrets to get Ben out of there. And now Lyman knows a *lot* more about what we know—which means that *his* army is already hard at work planning how to block *all* the moves I told him we'd be willing to make!"

Ben was able to follow what Jill had just said . . . but it was a perfect example of what he'd been feeling: *She* was able to see layers of planning and strategy in all this stuff that really didn't occur to him . . . not most of the time.

He was glad for Robert's support, but he didn't want to be the cause of more squabbling in the ranks.

"Really," he said quickly, "I promise I won't take off and do anything on my own again. I promise. But . . . you really do have to see the video and look at the faces of those guys when Jill was slicing them to bits—it was *awesome!*"

As those words left his mouth, Ben saw his favorite tiny half smile on Jill's lips . . . and he realized that maybe he wasn't so terrible at strategy after all—*some* kinds of strategy.

"Right, can't wait to see it," Robert said. "But *now*, it's time to deal with *that*," and he pointed at the package on Ben's desk.

Ben opened the desk drawer, got out a pair of small scissors, and handed them to Jill.

"You should do the honors . . . and Robert and

I can take pictures. I'll shoot video, and Robert, you take hi-res stills with the new camera, okay?"

Ben positioned the swing-arm of his desk lamp directly over the package, and then clicked the light to the brightest setting.

"Get a really tight picture of the seal, and then the stitching along both ends and the flap," Ben said.

"And also the fabric," Jill said. "That's canvas, right?"

"Yeah," Robert said, already snapping away. "Whoever did the sewing really knew what he was doing!"

"'What *he* was doing?'" said Jill. "You think a *man* sewed that?"

"Absolutely," Ben said. "In Captain Oakes's day, every sailor was an expert with a needle and twine— it was part of the job."

Jill flexed the scissors open and shut a few times.

"So . . . what's the best way to go after this thing?"

Ben said, "How about cutting each of the stitches along the right side so we can open that end. That'd do the least damage to it. Sound good?"

"Sounds good to me," Robert said. "Let 'er rip!"

"There will be *no* ripping," Jill said, "at all."

She got to work, then quickly realized she didn't have to snip each stitch. She cut every fourth or fifth one, then just pulled out a length of the heavy thread.

Ben followed the progress with his phone camera, pulling back once or twice to get Jill's face into the frame. Her nose got all scrunched up whenever she concentrated on something.

It took a little more than three minutes to get the end unstitched, and no one had to tell Jill what to do next. She pulled the layers of sailcloth open, and Ben aimed the desk lamp so it would shine inside.

There was a smaller package inside the cloth, and this one was wrapped in something that was the color of coffee.

"Robert, hang onto the left end," said Jill.

She reached into the open end with both hands and pulled, and the inner package slid out onto the desk. It was similar to the outer package, except its flap was held shut by *four* large globs of red sealing wax.

"Hmm . . . leather, don't you think?" Robert said.

"Yeah," said Ben, "it seems kind of brittle—hey! Check it out!"

He got in close with the camera, then quickly set it aside. There was an inscription on the flap of the packet, along with some kind of symbol. It was inked deep into the leather, like an old tattoo.

Robert read the words aloud:

Take this unopened to the nearest Grand Master

"That symbol? I've seen it before," Robert said.

"I've seen it too," said Jill. "It's used by Freemasons."

"Masons?" Ben thought a second. "Are those the guys who wear the strange hats and ride around on go-karts during the Fourth of July parade?"

"No," she said, "those are the Shriners. But Masons and Shriners are both fraternities, and they both use old-fashioned symbols."

"You mean after all this, we can't even *open* this thing?" Robert said.

"Well," Ben said, "not if we're going to follow Captain Oakes's orders exactly . . . and *I* think we should. I think we have to trust that he knew what he was doing. He says to take it 'unopened.' And also 'to the nearest Grand Master,' whatever that means."

"I know what it means," said Jill. "There's a Masonic lodge right here in Edgeport, over on Washington Street. And every lodge has a Grand Master. But if we follow the captain's directions *exactly*, it could be a problem."

"How come?" asked Robert.

"Because the Grand Master of that lodge is my dad."

CHAPTER 17

Bad Feeling

Tuesday night's emergency Keepers meeting continued early Wednesday morning in the school library. And Robert wasn't happy.

"I don't see why you won't just call your dad. Tell him there's a special delivery package for the Grand Master, and it's got to be opened right away—maybe he'd let you open it and tell him what you find. Because we're running out of time here. We can't just put everything on hold until he's back in town."

Jill shook her head. "We have to wait—he's back on Friday. It's bad enough that he has to get involved at all, but I'm sure not going to try to tell my dad about this stuff over the phone. He'll think I'm crazier than he already does."

"Jill's right," said Ben. "Her dad's the one who has to open that package, and that's all there is to it. So, we've just got to find other stuff to work on for a couple days."

"Yeah? Like what?" Robert sneered. "If we're gonna be so insanely careful about all the captain's stupid little rules, then we can't even look for the next safeguard until *this* one's all settled—right?"

"Well . . . ," Ben said slowly, "we can at least start *thinking* about the next clue. I don't see anything that would keep us from doing that." Then he added, "And if all else fails, we can go to our classes, and study for our last tests, and get all our final projects and reports finished—you know, school. And maybe if we back off a little, it'll give Lyman and Wally a false sense of security, and they'll get sloppy. Could be a good strategy."

Jill said, "Speaking of the dynamic duo, did you guys notice anything strange about them this morning, other than the fact that they were both here extra early? I mean, I was expecting some kind of reaction after the big showdown with Ben in the art room yesterday—I was pretty harsh over the phone. At the very least, I thought I'd see some anger today, especially from Wally. And there was nothing, hardly a frown from either one—barely a glance. And look"—she pointed toward the doors of the library—"nobody's even watching us. Seems weird, don't you think?"

Robert rolled his eyes. "First you get all freaked out when they follow you, and now you're worried because they're *not*?"

Jill narrowed her eyes, then spoke slowly and carefully. "All I am *saying*, Mr. Gerritt, is that this is a sudden change in enemy procedures. And we should pay attention, in case it *means* something."

Robert got up from the table. Mocking the way she'd just spoken, he said, "All *I* am saying, Miss Acton, is that *you* may pay all the attention you wish to those two lumps. *I* am going to go now, and finish earning straight As in all of my subjects. Have a *nice* day."

Jill kept her lips pressed tightly together until Robert was all the way out of the library, then spat out one word: "*Idiot!*"

Ben didn't want to try to defend Robert, and he realized he also didn't want to try to help Jill calm down. He didn't want to discuss what she'd said about Lyman and Wally, and he didn't want to discuss the clue for the next safeguard, or discuss anything at all.

There was really only one thing that he actually *wanted* to do, and it was so simple. He wanted to go sailing.

But he couldn't, not until Saturday.

"Listen, Jill, I'm gonna go to homeroom early, get some homework done. See you later, okay?"

"Yeah, fine."

She seemed glad to see him leave.

In the hallway outside the library, Ben took a quick look both ways, out of habit. No Lyman, no Wally.

He walked toward the front of the school and stopped when he had a clear view of the long front hallway that ran by the office. Again, neither man was in sight.

Curious now, he backtracked past the library doors, and near the north stairway he had a clear view across the other long hallway.

No Lyman, no Wally.

Walking briskly toward his homeroom, as he went past the causeway to the annex he glanced right. Nobody.

And when he rounded the corner and could see the whole south hallway, again neither man was in sight.

But he heard something: two men . . . laughing.

He walked along the hall until he was almost to the janitor's workroom, then bent down as if he was tying his shoe.

"Yeah," he heard Lyman say, "what a great game! And then we all went to that joint way out on East Fayette and ate that *super* hot chili! That was an *experience*!"

Wally laughed again, and then started trying to remember the name of a girl they'd both known.

Ben straightened up and tiptoed back toward the art room.

When he went in and sat down, Ms. Wilton saw him.

"Ben—good morning. You're in early today."

"Yeah, I wanted to check over some homework."

He got out a notebook and flipped it open, but he didn't even see the paper. He was thinking about what Jill had said.

Lyman and Wally *knew* that all three Keepers

were inside the school this morning, but they weren't tracking any of them. It was like they didn't care.

Ben knew a little about military strategy, and there were really just two main reasons why an enemy would ease up during a battle.

The first reason was pretty clear cut. If a commander had strong evidence that a battle was impossible to win, then it was time to stop throwing troops and resources at it. You might not actually start retreating or surrendering, but you stopped trying to make your troops advance.

That was one possibility—but how could that fit this situation? There was no way Glennley was going give up this fight, but that was how Lyman and Wally were acting suddenly. Like Jill said.

The second reason for backing off was a lot scarier to consider, and it made Ben tap his tongue on the back of his front teeth.

Because *sometimes* the commander of an army got hold of some special information. Maybe he knew about a secret weapon, or knew that a huge battalion of fresh troops was arriving, or that a massive air attack was coming, or even knew about a drastic change in the weather—but *whatever* this special knowledge was, it made the commander feel that victory was certain.

And if you were sure that victory was coming because of some *new* circumstance, then it made sense to ease up, and wait.

Ben had a bad feeling about this. *Something* was coming, something big.

And Lyman and Wally knew it.

CHAPTER 18

Brother to Brother

By Friday afternoon, the Keepers were in complete agreement: The two Glennley goons had apparently retired from spying, and they both seemed to be enjoying life as full-time school janitors. The building didn't appear to be any cleaner because of this sudden change, but the kids certainly experienced much more freedom of movement.

After observing Lyman and Wally relaxing early Wednesday morning, Ben had texted Jill.

Yr right about L n W—
they're not tracking anyone.
Could mean trouble. Talk later.

When all three of them had met at lunch Wednesday, Ben had laid out his theory— basically, that Lyman and Wally knew something was going to happen, something that would make whatever the Keepers did or didn't do completely unimportant.

Robert had said, "But how do you know it's not just a trick to get *us* to let our guard down?"

It was a good question, but when they had compared notes Wednesday after school, no one had been tracked or spied on—not once all day.

Even so, on Thursday Robert had checked out the entire school with their scanning device, just to be sure that Wally hadn't installed some supersecret surveillance system. He hadn't. The whole place was signal-free.

Then during lunch on Friday, all three of the Keepers had stood up and walked out of the cafeteria together, right under the noses of the Glennley men—an action that would have caused a major scramble just days earlier.

And neither Lyman nor Wally had shown any interest. They had even seemed mildly amused.

Ben really wished that the third safeguard business was completely settled, because with this kind of freedom, the search for safeguard number four could have been done so simply.

Ben felt more and more worried that some kind of Glennley plan was out there, like a ticking time bomb.

But for the moment, he'd managed to put all that out of his mind. He and Jill and Robert stood in the shade of a maple tree beside the parking lot of the Masonic lodge, and Tom Benton was just climbing out of a cab, right on time. Ben noticed that Tom wasn't using his walker today, just a sturdy aluminum cane.

The Harbor Light Lodge was a square, two-story brick building on Washington Street, less than half a mile from Oakes School. A small sign faced the parking lot, and it displayed that same symbol that was inked on the leather package in Ben's backpack. He had learned online that it was called the "square and compass," two tools that actual stonemasons used.

They walked over to the steps, and Tom said,

"Hi, kids. Looks like we're all here—everyone ready?"

"We've been ready for *days*!" Robert said.

"All right, then. Here we go!" And he pushed the button on the intercom next to the door.

Three seconds later a voice said, "Hi, Tom, and welcome! I'll be down in a minute—just take a seat in the foyer."

The door buzzed, and Tom pushed it open.

Tom took a chair next to an inner door, and Ben sat with Jill and Robert on a red cushioned bench along the wall. The place smelled funny to him—a mixture of men's cologne, wood smoke, and old floor wax.

Tom hadn't had any trouble setting up the meeting. He had called Jill's dad early Friday morning and said he'd been asked by a friend to bring an important looking package to the Grand Master of the Edgeport lodge. They'd agreed to meet at three forty-five—except Tom hadn't mentioned he was bringing three kids along. Ben wondered if that was going to be problem.

He whispered to Jill, "You ever been in here before?"

"It's a club for men only, Benjamin—they don't

do the bring-your-daughters-to-the-lodge thing."

"Men only?" Robert said. "Really? That's cave-man stuff."

"Yeah, well the Freemasons go back almost that far," said Jill. "Look 'em up online—you'll be amazed."

"So, like, how come your dad's into this?" Ben asked.

She shrugged. "The members are all from around this area, so I'm thinking it's partly for his business—networking and stuff. But they also do community work, like raising money for charities. From what I've read, there's nothing too weird about it—except for the men-only part."

There were footsteps from behind the door, and Tom stood up. Jill's dad came in and he stepped forward to shake hands.

"It's good of you to meet with me on such short notice, Mr. Acton."

"Call me Carl, and I'm glad you called. And I couldn't very well put off a meeting where someone's bringing me a mysterious package. Now, wh—"

He stopped mid-syllable when he saw the

kids—and then his daughter.

"*Jillie?* Wh-what are you doing you here, sweetheart?"

"It's kind of a long story, Daddy. Is there someplace we can all sit down?"

"Um . . . sure. Come on into the conference room."

They followed him through the door and past a wide wooden staircase. There was a red satin rope stretched across it, and Ben guessed that upstairs was where the members had their meetings.

The room they entered didn't look very lodge-like, as far as he could tell. There was a round wooden table with eight ordinary chairs around it. Bookcases filled one wall, and four or five posters about charity events covered another one. The one window in the room was large, but the panes were stained glass, alternating blue and gold. The seat Mr. Acton took faced west, and sometimes his face looked yellowish and sometimes it was tinted blue, like an old photograph.

He leaned forward onto his elbows and laced his fingers together. "So," he said, smiling across the table at his visitors, "if there's a long story about why you're here, someone better get it started."

Ben said, "It really begins back in the 1700s with Captain Oakes. You already know how he left a will, and how he wanted his building to always be a school, and how the town decided to buy out his heirs and sell everything to the Glennley Group. Well, the captain planned ahead, in case something like this ever happened. And he left things hidden around the school—he called them safeguards. He hoped they could be used to defend the school, to keep it for the kids and families of the town."

Mr. Acton lifted the pointer finger of his right hand. "And what do you kids have to do with this?"

Ben started by telling about the gold coin Mr. Keane had given him, and explained how its puzzle had led them to the large iron key and the instructions on the engraved copper plate, and the solemn oath that had made them the new Keepers of the School. He told about the codicil, about the gold and silver coins they'd discovered. As Ben mentioned each item, Robert and Jill used their iPads to show him the photos.

When Ben explained how the Underground Railroad hideout had actually been discovered,

Mr. Acton stared at Jill and the two boys.

"Are you saying that all of you have been *breaking into* the school? To hunt for these things?"

"We have keys, Daddy. Mr. Keane gave Ben his whole key ring before he died. And really, because of that new codicil, the Keepers actually *own* the school and all the land around it now—and you can't really break into a building that you already own, right?"

He frowned. "The codicil says that?"

Ben jumped in. "Whoever shows up in court and files the codicil is granted ownership."

"Well," he said, "I doubt if the police would see it that way. Go on, tell me the rest."

Ben started to explain how Mr. Lyman was actually working for Glennley and was using his fake job as janitor to spy on them, but Jill's dad immediately held up a finger. "This Lyman *spies* on you? What does that mean?"

Ben said, "He's a professional industrial spy. He's got all kinds of electronic equipment, and he's there to be sure that nothing upsets Glennley's plans at the last minute, before they tear down the school. And he's been tracking all of us, and not just around the school. He knows where each of us lives, and he even called my mom once, real late at night."

Mr. Acton jumped halfway out of his chair. "That is *outrageous*! I don't care what this fella does for a living! Any grown man who follows *my* daughter around is looking for a punch in the nose—and a call from my lawyer, and the chief of police, too!"

"It's not like we're in danger, Daddy," Jill said. "He just has to know where we are so he's sure we're not searching around the school."

Robert said, "Yeah, 'cause it didn't take Lyman long to figure out that we're hunting for things, except he still doesn't know what. And the Underground Railroad thing really scared them, because that could have gotten the whole building landmarked. So the best he can do is always try to keep an eye on us. He's got our class schedules, he knows where we live—we see him all over the place. And this week, he got a new man to help him out, a guy named Wally, another fake janitor."

"Well, I don't care what these men think they have to do," Mr. Acton growled. "Following kids around town is *way* out of bounds!"

Ben said, "Well, there's other stuff too. Because the people at Glennley keep feeding Lyman information about all of us. For example, if you left this meeting, and then tomorrow you sold those shares of Glennley stock you bought recently, Lyman would know all about that right away. And then the other side would guess that *you* knew something important—which is true. So really, you can't sell that stock, even if —"

"Hold it, hold it!" Mr. Acton's face was bright red. "How in *blazes* do you know about *my* stock trading?"

"Because Lyman told Jill and me about it one day in the school library—to make her feel bad about trying to stop the theme park, because that would make you lose money."

The man stroked his chin. "I don't *like* this Lyman guy, or his bosses. But they're sure right about the money. If this theme park project doesn't go through for Glennley, hard to tell how far their stock value would drop."

"Well," Ben said, "I think we can promise that you'll be repaid for everything you might lose on the stock by not selling your shares."

And then Ben glanced at Jill and Robert and

Tom. They all nodded.

Mr. Acton smiled like a dad. "That's a real sweet thing for all of you to say, but we're talking about *thousands* of dollars here, maybe even ten or fifteen grand. No, I'm a big boy, and besides, some stock losses are always handy at tax time."

"Daddy, you don't have to be all noble. Captain Oakes left a fund at Edgeport Bank and Trust, and the Keepers get to spend it on anything that helps keep the school safe. Like you not selling your stock right now."

Mr. Acton leaned forward. "A fund? You mean money?"

"It's a trust fund," said Ben. "Captain Oakes set it up, and the bankers have kept it going ever since 1791."

"So . . . how much are we talking about here?"

Jill said, "About eighty-eight million."

Her dad sat up straight. "No! Really? *Dollars? Eighty-eight million?"

Jill nodded. "And we can use as much as we need, to help protect the school."

The thought of all that money brought a wide smile to his face, followed by a sudden frown. "But I don't see how *I* fit into this . . . this puzzle."

Ben said, "We're just trying to follow the orders Captain Oakes left, Mr. Acton." He bent over and pulled the leather folder from his backpack and pushed it across the table. "This is the third safeguard we've found hidden inside the school, the package that Tom said he was bringing. And it's addressed to you. And right now, that's all we know about it."

"Addressed to *me*?" He read the inked inscription. "Ah . . . I see what you mean!" Mr. Acton smiled and nodded slowly. "I'm starting to think Captain Oakes must have been a pretty amazing guy. So let's see what he had on his mind."

Robert and Ben got out their cameras, but Mr. Acton said, "Sorry, fellas—no pictures, please. It's a lodge rule."

Without any ceremony, he took hold of the packet, slipped two fingers under the flap, and snapped all four of the red wax seals in about two seconds. When he opened the flap, the stiff leather cracked and then broke off. Ben winced to see such a great old artifact being treated like a mail-order package, but it was out of his hands.

The contents of the leather pouch were wrapped in some kind of dark blue cloth . . . at first Ben thought it might be a flag.

Mr. Acton pulled it out. "This is silk. And I'll bet this color was chosen on purpose."

There was no sealing wax, and Jill's dad simply unfolded the thin cloth. Ben found himself expecting some kind of treasure . . . diamonds would be nice.

"Hmm . . . three things in here," said Mr. Acton.

These had also been wrapped in colored silk—scarlet, green, and white. The scarlet fabric covered a lumpy looking object, and that was what he unwrapped first.

"Ah," Mr. Acton said, "a trowel!"

It looked like a pie server to Ben—except it appeared to be made of solid gold. Right away, Ben made the Masonic connection. He'd seen a workman use a tool like that to push mortar around when he was building a stone wall behind Ben's grandfather's cottage in Maine. But *this* trowel had obviously never been used for actual stonemasonry.

Mr. Acton held it up into a patch of yellow light and squinted. "Listen to this! 'To the Honourable Duncan Oakes, my dear Brother and Comrade-in-Arms.' And it's signed, 'from George Washington'! This . . . this is a chunk of real *history*, right here in my hands!"

Robert whispered, "Open the little green one next—I mean, *please* open it."

Mr. Acton smiled. He set the trowel down on its scarlet cloth and reached for the small green bundle.

When he pulled back the covering, Jill reacted first.

"That is *beautiful*!"

She was right. It was a round red jewel, as big as a quarter, set in the center of a golden sunburst. Three diamonds glittered on a wide gold loop above the jewel, and a green silk ribbon, the same

color as the silk wrapping, ran through the loop.

Mr. Acton stood up quickly and went to pull a book from the shelf behind Tom Benton.

"I've heard of these, but I've never actually seen one—at least, not a real one."

He turned to the index, then flipped to a page near the middle of the book. He held the book so they all could see a color photograph. It showed an item almost identical to the piece of jewelry on the desk. He read the caption.

"'Dating from Scotland in the early 1700s, this red jewel sunburst, suspended from a green collar-ribbon, confers honour upon a Brother who has proven a special affinity for protecting and renewing all that is good upon the earth.' Pretty amazing, eh? And I bet that's a twenty-carat ruby right there—probably worth a *bundle*!"

"Open the last one, Daddy."

Ben thought Jill seemed a little embarrassed by her father's interest in how much the jewel was worth, but it seemed perfectly normal to him—after all, this was a treasure hunt.

But Ben was instantly disappointed with the final item. The white silk unfolded to reveal a triangle of pale leather with a bold black border and a couple of marks or drawings on it. There were thin red ropes attached to two of the corners. It reminded Ben of a signal pennant.

Mr. Acton was more excited about this than either of the other things.

"Do you *believe* this? This is just . . . awesome! *Awesome!*"

Tom Benton said, "My father was a Freemason, and I've got a photo of him wearing something like that. It's a ceremonial apron, right?"

"Exactly," said Mr. Acton.

Ben leaned in for a closer look, and he had to admit that the designs on the thing were pretty cool. They'd been done with fancy sewing and embroidery, and there were all sorts of little flags

and symbols and shapes, even some animals. Plus a two-headed eagle up at the top. And it looked like there were tiny pearls and maybe even some diamonds and bits of gold worked into the pictures.

Mr. Acton said, "I know this won't mean much to you, but this tells me that Captain Oakes was a thirty-second degree Mason—which back in his day may have been even more significant than it is today. It all probably looks a little strange, maybe even kind of silly. But there's no mystery about any of this. A Masonic lodge is really just a bunch of guys who keep telling each other that they can do more than they're already doing, and be better people than they already are. And if the brothers in your lodge keep voting for you to advance through the different degrees, and they eventually move you up to the highest—the thirty-second degree—it means they all agree that you're a really good person in just about every way they can think of. So, hats off to Captain Oakes! And the workmanship on this apron is really something—it'd probably fetch a pretty penny on eBay!"

He lifted the apron gently by its top corners, and when he did, Ben saw something drop to the floor. It was a sheet of vellum, a perfect square about six inches across—with writing on it.

Robert picked it up, but didn't read it. He handed it to Jill's dad and said, "This is for you."

Ben watched Mr. Acton's eyes as he read the message. His lips moved slightly as he did, and then he read it aloud.

"'Dear Brother:

My trusted friends have brought you these gifts as a token of my respect.

Please offer them every assistance within your power.

With everlasting thanks,

Captain Duncan Oakes'"

It was quiet for a long moment. Mr. Acton wasn't getting weepy or anything, but Ben could tell he was deeply moved.

Robert broke the silence.

"So, I get all the rigamarole about the degrees, and I like the fancy stuff he gave you and everything, but was it really so important for *you* to open this up instead of us? Why did he want it to happen like this?"

Mr. Acton set down the vellum sheet and

folded his hands on the table. He looked from face to face, and Ben had never heard anyone speak so solemnly.

"Captain Oakes wanted it this way because now this is a matter between him and me, directly. I am bound to keep all of his secrets until the day I die, and all of your secrets too. I am bound by my sacred honor as a Freemason and a man to do all I can to help him, and he has asked me to do just one thing—to help *you* in every way I can. From this moment forward, I'm ready to march in your army, and all I need are my orders. So, who's in charge here?"

Jill spoke right up. "We're all working together, but if you put it like that, it's Ben, Daddy. Ben's in charge."

Ben was shocked. He started to blush, and almost contradicted her. But just as quickly the thought came, Well, *technically*, she's right. Mr. Keane gave me the gold coin, so that's where the chain of command starts.

Out loud, he said, "Jill just means that I was the first one to begin working on all this. We really try to make decisions as a team, but *I* definitely think you should be the chief business officer. In the last couple days we started a new battle with Glennley—outside the school. And it's *way* beyond what any of us know about. But our lawyer can explain it."

His eyebrows shot up. "You kids have your own lawyer?"

Ben nodded. "His name is Harold Chamden."

Mr. Acton smiled. "Harry and I are good friends. Should I give him a call?"

Ben said, "The sooner the better."

"Great, can't wait!"

Mr. Acton's face was flushed, and he jumped up and hurried around the table, shaking everyone's hand. When he got to Jill, he gave her a big hug.

"I'm awfully proud of you, Jillie!" Sensing her embarrassment, he quickly added, "And all of you— amazing stuff! Whew!" He got out a handkerchief and mopped his forehead, then pulled off his suit coat and went to the window. He pushed it up about ten inches, then put his face into the fresh air and took a few deep breaths.

"Whooh, that's better! Hot in here, don't you think?" Glancing outside, he said, "Looks like somebody's ride home is here."

Ben walked to the window, and what he saw

was a surprise.

"See the man in that truck, Mr. Acton? *That* is Jerroald Lyman. For the past few days he hasn't seemed very interested in us, but I guess our meeting here must have made him curious."

Jill's dad took a long hard look, then muttered, "So, that fella thinks he's going to spy on *me* now, is that it?"

Ben smiled grimly. "Welcome to the Keepers of the School."

CHAPTER 19

Race Day

"Have a wonderful race, sweetheart, and I'll see *you* at the trophy presentation!"

"What? Oh . . . right." Ben grinned at her. "Thanks, Mom."

He got out of the car and hoisted his duffel bag onto one shoulder and his book bag onto the other.

Having his own boat had changed the Saturday routine. Instead of taking him directly to the sailing club at half past noon, his mom had driven him to Parson's Marina at ten thirty. That way, he'd have time to eat an early lunch with his dad, then launch his boat from the storage lockers at the marina beach. And from there he would have to sail it south to the beach at the club so he could sign in and go through the equipment check.

His mom didn't drive off until Kevin had buzzed him through the gate by the security shed.

Like I'm six years old or something!

He quickly felt bad for thinking that. It was good to have a mom who wanted to be sure you were safe. Good . . . but still annoying.

She hadn't said anything, but Ben could tell his mom didn't like the new race-day arrangement. It meant she had to hand him over to his dad earlier than the time in their agreement.

Like she's being cheated out of two-and-a-half precious hours with wonderful me!

Then he felt bad for thinking that, too. Saturday was house-switching day, and it always bothered his mom even more than it bothered him—or his dad. The whole separation thing wasn't getting any easier.

He went to the window of the security shed.

"Hi, Kevin. I'm taking my new boat out in about an

hour, so I'll need the key to the storage shed. You gonna be here awhile? Or should I take the key now?"

"Better take it now. Got a big provisioning job this afternoon—a lot of deliveries coming, and I promised the owner I'd check all the receipts." Kevin nodded toward the concrete pier just beyond the gas dock. "That's the boat—and she's a real beauty."

Ben looked, and Kevin was right. The mast shot up seventy-five or eighty feet above the waterline. The largest sailboats at Parson's were usually forty or forty-five feet long. This one was bigger.

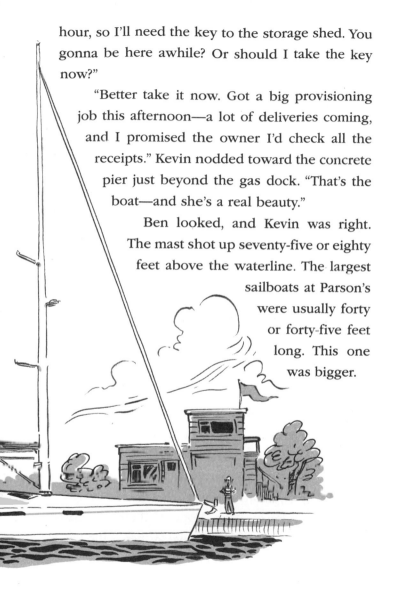

"Wow! Is that a Beneteau?"

"Nope, it's a Jeanneau 57, only a few years old. And it's got all the bells and whistles—bow thrusters, self-furling headsail and genoa, twin helms—a real pip. And the fella who brought her in last Saturday? He sailed it here and docked it *single-handed*—laid it in that berth like droppin' a slice of bread into a toaster!"

Ben was gawking now—the hull had such clean, graceful lines. This yacht made the *Tempus Fugit* look like a toy.

"Have you been onboard?" he asked Kevin.

"Me?" He chuckled. "Nope, but ask your dad. Yesterday about sunset he got the grand tour from the owner himself. It's that same fella your girlfriend asked me about, the man who was looking to buy your dad's boat a couple weeks ago."

Ben had trouble making his mouth work. *"Who?"*

"Tall skinny guy," said Kevin, "doesn't smile much. But he's real generous with his tips, I'll say that much. Says if I help him get squared away to sail for the Bahamas by Monday, there'll be two hundred bucks in it for me! Anyway, here's the key."

"The what?" said Ben. His ears weren't working either.

"The key," Kevin repeated, "to the storage shed."

"Right—thanks." He took the key and started to turn away, still replaying what Kevin had said. He stopped quickly. "That girl you mentioned? She's not my girlfriend."

Kevin winked at him. "Well, she oughta be!"

Ben didn't react to that—he barely heard it. He was already hurrying onto the floating pier, out toward the *Tempus Fugit*.

He was trying to pull the facts from what Kevin had said, get them straight in his mind. He was also trying to remember to breathe. And not walk off the pier into the water.

Fact one: That huge French sailboat? The owner was Jerroald Lyman—he recalled Jill had said Lyman was rich and owned a big boat. She'd learned that at the same time she figured out Lyman worked for the Glennley Group.

Fact two: His *dad* had been on board that boat with Lyman! Ben wasn't sure what that meant, but it creeped him out anyway. First, that sleazy real estate guy talking with his mom, and now *this*? It might be just a coincidence—but Ben had stopped believing in coincidences. If Glennley was involved, it was happening for a purpose—a bad one.

Fact three: Lyman was planning to sail away, to leave Edgeport on Monday—*this* Monday! Ben couldn't make sense of that. But if Kevin was right, then that meant Lyman was *sure* that his work here would be done by Monday. *Monday!*

Fact four: That boat had arrived in Edgeport last Friday . . . and it had been sailed single-handed! But that meant . . .

Ben dropped his duffel and pack onto the walkway and ran back to the security shed.

"Hey, Kevin, was it the owner who sailed that boat in here on Friday?"

"Nope, it was a short stocky guy. But you shoulda seen him setting the bumpers alongside as the boat eased to—that little fella can *move*!"

Ben said, "Thanks."

He turned and walked slowly back to the things he'd dropped.

Fact five: It was *Wally* who had sailed Lyman's boat into port! He'd arrived on Friday—just in time to help Lyman shoot a secret video at school early

Saturday morning . . . and then report for work on Monday as the new assistant janitor.

Ben stood over his duffel and backpack, but he didn't pick them up. He took out his phone—once he got to his dad's boat, there'd be no way to talk privately. And he had to tell Jill and Robert about this right now—so they couldn't accuse him of working all on his own. And also so they could help him figure out what these facts *meant*—especially the part about leaving on Monday—the day after tomorrow!

What do Lyman and Wally know?

He lit up the screen on his phone.

They know something—that's why they backed off at school this week.

He clicked to the menu.

What is *it? What's coming?*

He was ready to push the talk button. But he didn't.

Did Lyman and Wally find something else in the art supplies room—I'm sure they searched in there after I left on Tuesday. . . .

He clicked to the picture gallery on his phone and looked at every single photo he'd taken in the supplies room.

What am I missing?

And then he saw it, right there on his phone.

But it wasn't a photo.

It was a number, the numeral 1, right there next to the voice memo app.

Because when he'd been in that supplies room Tuesday after school, he had heard Lyman and Wally arguing in the janitor's room, heard their voices right through the wall.

And he'd done something about that, something smart.

He had made a recording.

CHAPTER 20

Garbled

"Hey, sailor! All set for the race?"

"What? Oh, yeah—I'm psyched!"

His dad stood at the stove cooking up spaghetti for lunch. As Ben edged through the boat's tiny galley, he had to be careful that his duffel bag didn't knock the empty sauce jar off the counter.

"You know, we could use the car to tow your boat over to the club, and you could launch it there."

"Thanks . . . ," Ben said slowly, "but I'd rather sail it over."

"Okay, then. Food'll be ready in about twenty minutes—should leave plenty of time to get you onto the water by noon or so."

"Sounds great, Dad. Thanks."

Ben walked calmly to his tiny cabin at the bow of the boat and softly closed the door, but his mind was running so fast he almost couldn't stand it.

With shaky hands he pulled out his phone and punched up the summary screen for Voice Memo 1.

Date: June 1
Time: 3:44 p.m.

He already knew that.

But the next bit was a surprise.

Duration: 47 seconds

Can that be right?

It had felt like he'd stood there with his phone pressed against that wall for at least five minutes . . . before that brass coffin lid had clanged to the floor.

He plugged earbuds into his phone, and pushed play.

Nothing sounded clear, but it certainly seemed

like two different voices—and of course that meant Lyman's and Wally's. And the vibe coming through that wall from the janitor's workshop made him pretty sure that this wasn't a friendly chat—it was an argument. With yelling.

But the sound quality was terrible. It was sort of like both men were talking underwater, or maybe had their mouths stuffed with marshmallows. Only one sound was sharp and clear—the huge *bong* at the end.

There was also a steady high-pitched hum . . . and a low buzzing rumble, too. And the volume level kept rising and falling—it was like being at his grandparents' place in Maine and listening to a Red Sox game on an AM radio station.

He'd watched enough cop shows to know that there were ways to start with bad sound and make it better, to clean it up—but he didn't happen to have the FBI crime lab to help him out.

I wonder what Robert would do?

Ben was *not* happy with that thought.

He took an instant inventory, and then changed his question.

I've got my laptop, an iPad, a good set of earphones, a strong Wi-Fi connection, and about twenty minutes—how can I fix this lousy voice memo?

That simple question helped, and a course of action snapped into focus.

First, Ben clicked back to the menu screen on his phone, highlighted "Voice Memo 1," and then e-mailed it—to himself.

He sat at his desk, pulled his laptop from his backpack, and opened it up. It took thirty seconds to start, and then another ten seconds for his e-mail program to load. During that time he found his good earphones in his desk and plugged them into the computer. He clicked "Get Messages" . . .

Yes!

He had a new e-mail from himself, with an audio attachment: "Voice Memo 1." So now the memo was just like any other sound file on his computer!

He dragged the memo file out of the e-mail and dropped it onto the iTunes icon. Instantly, the memo began playing through his headphones. The sound quality wasn't really better—he just heard more clearly how awful it was.

But he'd used iTunes a lot, and he knew

how to change the way a song sounded—which seemed worth a try.

First he selected the memo in the iTunes list, then clicked on "File," then "Get Info," which opened up a window on his screen. And in that window, he clicked on the "Options" button. There was a slider button to change the loudness of the memo, so he bumped it up—making it louder couldn't hurt, right?

Fortunately, he remembered the huge *bong* at the end, and he used the "Stop Time" setting to cut off the final two seconds of the memo.

But what he really wanted to use were the "Equalizer Preset" choices. He clicked open the list, and selected "Spoken Word."

Then he listened to the memo again—without the big clang at the end this time.

It wasn't any clearer.

Hmm . . . research!

He opened an Internet browser window and typed in "fixing a bad recording." A lot of garbage showed up, but about ten items down from the top, something caught his eye—an IPad app called Gottahearit.

Ben reached into his pack again and

pulled out the iPad. He knew how to use the App Store, and thanks to Robert's planning, the Keepers already had an account that was linked to their credit card at Edgeport Bank and Trust.

A quick search in the App Store brought up the info about Gottahearit. It was a sound filtering program, with lots of ways to choose specific parts of a recording and either cut them out, or make them louder and clearer. And at a price of $4.99, it was certainly worth a shot. He clicked "Purchase," entered the account password, and in fifteen seconds the new app appeared on the screen in his hands.

It took him a few minutes to locate the e-mail he'd sent himself, import the voice memo into iTunes on the iPad, and then move it from iTunes to the new application.

But once the memo was there in the Gotta-

hearit window, everything became much simpler. The whole forty-five seconds of audio was laid out across the screen as a picture of the sound waves. It looked like a little mountain range, with lots of peaks and valleys.

And all he had to do was go through the recording and pick which kinds of sounds to keep, and which kinds to block. He identified Lyman's voice waves and Wally's voice waves, and put them onto the "Keep" list. He identified the high hum waves, and the low buzz waves, and put them onto the "Zap" list. Then he pushed a button to even out the volume level, and two other buttons labeled "enhance voice tones" and "Filter Noise."

After five minutes he was able to hear some words—kind of.

And he was able to get an idea what the men had been arguing about—kind of.

But it was still garbled.

He got out a notecard, and as the memo played, he wrote down the words and phrases he could hear—kind of.

He also added an *L* or *W* to show who had said what.

in charge L
chief (maybe <u>thief</u>) W
boss (maybe <u>loss</u>) L
quickest way around (or maybe <u>down</u>) W
just forget it (or <u>just go get it</u>?) L
shrink (or maybe <u>stink</u>) L
remember who (or maybe <u>to</u>) L
shuttle [something] talents (or maybe <u>balance</u>?) L
shuttle topple [something]
twenty flowers? L
sunk (or maybe <u>shrunk</u> or <u>skunk</u>?) L
sweat? slow today (or <u>saw today</u>?) W
all over by Monday L

Lyman's last phrase was chillingly clear, and Ben hated writing the words—it looked so harsh and final: all over by Monday.

"Food's ready, Ben."

"There in a minute," he called back.

Jill and Robert *really* had to know about this now. And listen to the memo, too.

He saved his cleaned-up sound file and then copied it into a new e-mail. He added Jill's and Robert's e-mail addresses, then wrote:

Lyman's boat is at Parson's marina—he's leaving for a long trip MONDAY! Must have some kind of plan—it's why he and W slacked off this week.
Listen to the recording I made it Tuesday— best sound I can give you, L n W arguing.
Don't know if there are any real clues here or not.
Text me right away if you have ideas.
Ben

He started to put away the iPad, but there was an immediate reply from Robert.

Nice try, Pratt!
Classic prerace brain attack—not buying it.
Today you lose!
Captain Gerritt

Ben started to reply, but just shook his head and put the iPad to sleep.

What an idiot!

But maybe that idiot, who was also a genius, would listen to the recording anyway. And get an idea.

At this point it was out of his hands—at least for a few hours.

He had spaghetti to eat.

And then he had a race to win.

CHAPTER 21

Bright Sun, Dark Clouds

It was a little after one p.m., and the observation deck of the Bluewater Sailing Club was the perfect spot for some last minute research. One look across the bay told Ben that today's race would be tough.

The course lay about half a mile offshore, and three big red buoys made a triangle. The longest side was about three-fourths of a mile long, and the two short sides were about a quarter mile each—and the race was two full laps.

A steady fourteen-knot breeze was blowing up

out of the southeast, but the water wasn't choppy. Instead, long sets of two- and three-foot swells swept through the course. Making clean turns was going to be hard, and it was going to take a different set of skills at each buoy.

Like the last race—the one where Robert had nearly drowned—the two of them had both drawn the second racing group. Ben had made the short voyage from his home beach, gotten his boat checked in and prepped on the club beach, and then he'd hurried to the clubhouse to watch the first twelve Optimists beat their way around the course.

In just ten minutes of the first lap, he saw six different sailors miss a turn, and four of those had happened at the farthest downwind buoy.

Tough course! And the laps'll go fast.

But Ben still smiled as he watched—if they'd made the course easy, it wouldn't be half as fun. He leaned forward against the wooden railing, totally lost in the action.

"Thought you'd be getting set to launch by now!"

"Dad—hi!" Ben smiled, but he didn't take his eyes off the boats. "Just checking out the course.

Um . . . did you see Mom yet? When she dropped me off she said—"

He felt a tap on his shoulder.

"I'm already here! Your father and I made plans a week ago to come and watch your new boat in action. But if he hadn't said hello, I don't think you'd have noticed either one of us. It's a *perfect* day for sailing, don't you think?"

She sounded happy. Ben smiled and said, "Yeah, unless you want to try to win a race. And as long as you don't mind freezing a little."

He'd gotten thoroughly wet on his way to the sailing club, and the water wasn't much warmer than it had been three weeks ago.

But his mom was sure right about the way everything looked. Sails of all sizes dotted the brilliant blue waters, from the inner harbor all the way out past the headlands, where a stronger wind was kicking up whitecaps.

Ben glanced over toward the beach. The launch marshal had just lifted the Preparatory flag. He had to go check in, but he didn't want to. He wanted to stay right where he was, there between his mom and dad—stay and watch the races together, maybe sit at a table all afternoon and then order some burgers.

But his dad knew the signal flags too.

"Looks like you need to get over to the beach, Ben."

"Yeah, I do. Well, I'll see you afterwards, okay?"

"You bet, sweetheart," his mom said. "And be careful, all right?"

"I will, Mom."

"And good luck out there!" his dad said.

Ben looked at him. "I heard a quote a while ago: 'Shallow men believe in luck . . . Strong men believe in cause and effect.' Ralph Waldo Emerson said it, and I think it's true."

Ben had a sudden thought that made him cringe, and even blush a little.

I think I just sounded like Robert!

His dad nodded thoughtfully. "I like it." Then he smiled and said, "And I heard a quote about twenty years ago, written by John Paul Jones: 'I wish to have no connection with any ship that does not sail fast, for I intend to go in harm's way.' So, go hop into your fast ship, and let's see some great cause and effect out there!"

"And stay *out* of harm's way!" his mom added. She smiled, but Ben knew she was serious.

"Thanks. I'll be careful *and* fast! See you guys later!"

The start for the second group of boats was delayed. The wind had shifted, so two of the buoys needed to be repositioned. When Ben shoved off from the club beach, he had to set a three-tack course to reach the starting line.

Another boat pulled close downwind, mostly hidden by his sail. But Ben already knew who it was. If Robert had any fears after almost drowning during their last race, they sure weren't showing today.

"Ahoy there, Pratt! I hope you feel like losing today, because I sure feel like making that happen!"

Ben ignored the taunt, and called back, "Did you listen to that file I sent? It wasn't a joke, Gerritt. Lyman's really thinking his work is all done here, and he's pulling out Monday."

"Yeah, I listened—it's really hard to hear anything clearly, Pratt. Besides, maybe Lyman's talking about some other Monday, or even some other issue entirely—ever think of that? That recording could mean a million different things. *You* need to put all that out of your puny little mind, because I need you to focus on losing this race!"

Instead of replying, Ben pulled in his sheet and quickly came about. In three seconds there was a nice stretch of water between them. Conversation over.

In a way, though, Robert was right—except for the digs about losing.

Because Ben didn't want to think about any of that stuff now. He just wanted to sail his new boat—which he loved. Compared to other boats he'd been stuck with for races, this one handled like a sports car, and it rode the swells like a surfboard.

Just as he made ready to come about for his last tack to the starting buoy, a tall sail a quarter mile northward caught his eye.

It was the big Jeanneau yacht, and there at the port-side wheel Ben could see Lyman himself, his face tilted upward, checking the trim of the headsail. And there was Wally, too, working one of the winches just fore of the helm. Both of them were wearing white trousers and sport shirts— two gentleman janitors out for a Saturday sail.

Ben pulled his Optimist onto its new line, and

a sharp flash of anger stabbed at him—the idea of those two cruising around on a half-million-dollar boat!

That moment of inattention cost his boat a sudden dig into the side of a swell, and he shipped about five gallons of cold seawater. Bailing like mad, he kept his eyes ahead and his bow aimed for the starting mark—and he pushed Lyman and Wally completely out of his mind.

The Optimist flag and the Preparatory flag had both been hoisted at the stern of the race officer's boat, and Ben hadn't marked the time—another error.

But judging by where Robert was positioned, there was probably about a minute before the Optimist flag would drop and the air horn would signal the start.

So he was still in good shape.

He bailed out one last scoop of water and slid forward to trim the hull. He was locked in on the mark now, and he saw a perfect path to the starting line. He nudged the tiller and pulled on the sheet—but suddenly something felt wrong.

It was his phone, vibrating in the waterproof chest pocket of his life vest.

Electronics of any kind were forbidden onboard during a race, but he'd thought Jill might try to call him after listening to that recording. And he wasn't going to use his phone to try to cheat or something, so he'd brought it.

He pulled the sheet into a cleat, which freed up his left hand. Then he reached into the pocket, pushed the talk button, and then the speaker control.

"Talk to me!" he barked, and yanked the rope loose from the cleat just in time to ease up and avoid a collision.

"Well, a friendly hello to you to!" Jill said.

"Louder," he shouted. "Get anything useful?"

A younger girl in a boat less than ten feet away looked at Ben like he'd gone mad and was talking to himself—or even worse, talking to her.

Jill spoke up, and Ben could hear her.

"Only a few words really seem clear to me, but I don't know what they mean."

"Tell me!" he yelled.

The little girl was doing all she could to get her boat farther away from Ben's.

Jill paused, then said, "Hey—you're sailing, right? And the race is starting! How much time do I have?"

"Almost none! Just the important words! Tell me!" he bellowed.

The little girl looked terrified. "I don't *know*!" she wailed. "Stop yelling at me!"

Ben felt sorry, but he had to ignore her because Gerritt was making a move, trying to use that Rule Eleven leeward gambit, trying to force him to give way and lose his line.

With barely a thought, Ben jogged his tiller, which instantly blocked Gerritt's wind and dropped him two lengths back.

Jill's voice was faint and tinny, but Ben heard her.

"I'm pretty sure I heard the word 'scuttle,' and I definitely heard 'Saturday.' And there's something about 'talents'—or it might be 'gallons.' And then 'all over by Monday.'"

"Okay—gotta go! Thanks!" Ben grabbed the sheet with his teeth, which he shouldn't have done—he had caps on the front two. But he was able to grip the rope for half a second, just long enough to tap his chest pocket and end the phone call.

At that moment, the flag dropped—*rheeeeehp!*

And as the blast from the air horn faded, Ben

crossed the line very close to the mark—one of the best starts he'd ever made!

But he was barely aware of it.

His mind was back aboard the *Tempus Fugit*, running through his list of possible words on that index card, trying to *see* each one—and trying to match his list with what Jill had just said.

She said "Saturday"—and I had "slow today" or "saw today"—which could be Saturday. Okay, Saturday—which is today!

This first leg of the race was one of the short sides of the triangle, and it aimed east-southeast . . . which meant that Ben had to keep his bow just a few points off the wind. He found a sweet line and held to it, almost without effort—except he had to do a lot of weight shifting to compensate for the swells.

I thought I heard "shuttle," and Jill heard "scuttle." So that works. But both words have possibilities . . . and Lyman might have been talking about his boat.

Because Ben knew what Jill's word meant. If you scuttled a boat, it meant you sank it on purpose, like during a sea battle to block a shipping channel or the entrance to a harbor. Or if you needed to put an enemy ship completely

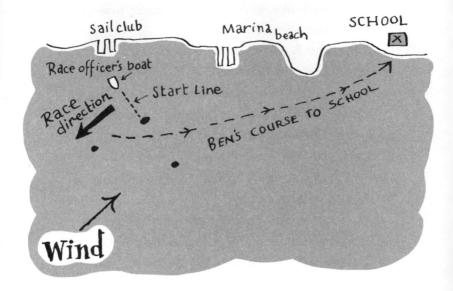

out of commission, you went down below the waterline and you opened all the sea valves, which would let the water come rush—

Water!—"gallons," *not "talents" or "balance"! Gallons of water!*

Lyman was going to scuttle the school! Saturday!

Ben jammed his tiller hard right, and instantly the bow jumped left.

The windward boat nearest behind him was Gerritt's, and Robert shouted, "Clear! Clear!"

It looked like a collision for sure. But the boom whizzed above Ben's head, the sail snapped tight, and his boat leaped forward out of Robert's path—with just inches to spare.

It was a textbook move, a perfect snap turn—but at the wrong place. It also put his boat onto the exact course Ben wanted: north-northwest, and toward the shore. More accurately, right toward the Oakes School.

"Pratt!" Gerritt yelled. "You're in violation!"

Robert was right, of course.

Because Ben was now sailing straight through the middle of the triangle defined by the three race buoys—a clear violation.

The air horn chirped, and he glanced at the race officer's boat—a black-and-yellow flag waved at him.

Ben ignored the warning and frowned at his sail.

It's gonna take thirty minutes to reach the school—too long!

He reached for the halyard, gave a pull, and let his sail drop into the hull. The boat lost headway, gently rolling with the swell. One of the race boats began motoring toward him.

He got out his phone, clicked to Jill's number, and punched talk.

It began to ring.

Pick up, Jill! You've gotta do something now!

The phone kept ringing.

C'mon, Jill—answer! You have *to!*

And on the sixth ring, she did.

CHAPTER 22

Like Family, Like Enemies

Jill said, "This is what I've got so far—do you want to hear?"

Ben and Robert nodded, and she began reading from a document on her iPad.

> *At approximately two o'clock on Saturday afternoon, firefighters used axes to break open a side door at the Oakes School. They were responding to a 911 call about a fire on the third floor.*
>
> *But when the fire crew charged*

up the stairs, they didn't find a fire.

What they found was a flood.

In the third-floor girls' room, a pipe had broken, one of those big silver pipes attached to a toilet. It wasn't clear whether a gasket had failed, or if the old pipe had corroded away. But whatever the cause, one thing was clear: For at least one hour, water had been gushing out at about fifty gallons per minute.

A former Oakes School janitor, a man named Tom Benton, was near the school and noticed the fire trucks. When he learned what the problem was, he went right to the school basement and turned off the main water valve to the building.

There was a large drain in the center of the tile floor in the girls' room, so only about half of the three-thousand gallon flood had gotten out into the hallway.

Mr. Lyman, the present school janitor, did not respond to his phone or his emergency beeper, so the firefighters and some citizen volunteers who appeared on the scene did what they could to deal with the water. People used mops and buckets, towels from the gymnasium, and two large water vacuums owned by the school.

There was some damage to the wooden floors in the third-floor hallway, and the plaster ceiling in the second floor hallway was also spotted and dripping. Four computers in a lab on the second-floor were destroyed by water.

One of the firefighters said that if it had been Monday morning before the flooding was discovered, the entire basement of the school would have filled up like a swimming pool, and water would have risen up to about three feet in all the rooms on the first floor. Also, most of the ceilings in the second- and first-floor classrooms would have gotten soggy and fallen to the floor, and all the books in the school library would have been destroyed, including the original books left by Captain Oakes. And the Underground Railroad station under the north staircase would have been completely flooded.

The fire chief said that if the flooding had not been stopped when it was, town inspectors probably would have had to declare the whole building unsafe. And certainly, no students would have been permitted inside the building. They would have had to finish the last few days of the school year somewhere else.

And the 911 call that saved the school? It came from an untraceable cell phone.

"So, what do you think?" she asked.

"It's *awesome*," Ben said. He especially liked all the things she'd left out—about how he had called her, and how she had been the one who called 911 and Tom Benton.

Robert nodded in agreement, then said, "Yeah, it's a good summary, but what's it for?"

"Well," Jill said, "at the very least, I can use it as

part of our project on the history of the school—it's a pretty important historical moment, don't you think? And I thought I might send it to the *Edgeport Pennant* tomorrow—let them do whatever they want with it—publish it, or just use it for information if they write a story of their own."

"What do you mean 'if'!" Ben exclaimed. "You *know* they're gonna do a big story about this!"

It was Sunday afternoon and they were sitting on the seawall in front of the school, looking out at the water. It wasn't really a Keepers meeting—just a chance to catch up about the recent events.

They were also taking a rest, because they were part of a flash mob that the Historical Society and the PTA had organized to help clean up the school before Monday morning—eighty or ninety people had shown up.

Which was good, because there was a lot to do, much more than the school janitors could do on their own. Both Lyman and Wally had worked from Saturday evening until almost two in the morning under the direct supervision of Mr. Telmer, the principal. And they probably had another late night coming up.

The broken pipe had been repaired, and the

school's water system had been checked by a team of plumbers. Every last bit of water had been vacuumed, squeegeed, soaked up, and removed. And now huge industrial fans were all over the school, evaporating the last of the moisture from the floors and walls and ceilings.

Jill said, "I'm not including it in the report, of course, but what did you tell your mom and dad about the race and everything?"

Robert butted in. "I can answer that—Ben told his mommy and daddy that he realized there was no way he was *ever* going to beat me in a sailing race, so he used this emergency as a way to disqualify himself and save face! Classic move, Pratt!"

"Very funny," said Ben. "Remember, *you're* the idiot who said that the recording I made was useless." Ben paused a moment, then looked Jill in the eye. "What I told my mom and dad? I told them the truth."

Jill scrunched up her nose. "You mean . . . ?"

"I mean I told them everything," Ben said. "I couldn't keep lying to them about this stuff. I know I didn't get anyone's approval, and I'm sorry about that. But I figured, if your dad can be trusted, then my mom and dad can be part of the team too. And I especially had to tell my mom. She had to know about the real estate thing, how Glennley was trying to use her. You should have seen my dad get mad about that—it was great!"

Ben's face reddened at his own burst of emotion there, but Jill covered for him.

"So . . . her feelings weren't hurt about it?"

"A little, but she totally got it. And when I told my dad everything about the man who owns the yacht he toured on Friday night? It blew his mind! So anyway, we should tell the others that there are two more Keepers."

"Um . . . *three* more Keepers," said Jill "My dad and I decided that we had to tell my mom—it was his idea. And it took twenty minutes and a lot of photos to convince her we weren't making it all up just to tease her."

"Well, isn't this *cozy*," Robert snapped. "A real *family* affair. All I have to do now is tell Gram, and then we can all have a big Keepers of the School *family* picnic!"

The icy sarcasm chilled the air.

"It's . . . it's not like that, Robert—" Ben began. Robert cut him off.

"Easy for *you* to say!"

Another deep freeze.

But Jill wasn't having it.

"Your mom and dad died, Robert—we get it, and we're sorry, but it's not our fault. Or your fault either."

Ben barely breathed, amazed at Jill's bravery . . . or was she just going for the throat—a killer?

She wasn't done.

"And you *should* tell your grandmother, Robert—that's my vote. Because it *is* a family thing, all of this is—the school, the harbor, the town, everything we're trying to protect. And the three of us, too. It's a family thing, so stop acting like *you* don't have one. Because it's not true."

It took a moment, but the universe unfroze and then stayed that way.

Robert found it hard to look into their faces.

But he did, and even smiled a little.

"Sorry. And you're right about the family stuff, all of it. And . . . I want to say something else. No matter how all this turns out in the next week or so, it's still gonna be one of the best times of my whole life. I've never had so much fun . . . and I've never had guys like you around either."

"Like family," Jill said.

"Exactly," said Ben, "like family . . . only a *lot* goofier!"

That didn't get a big laugh, but it was enough to ease the tension.

Ben said, "Look, we should get back inside and help finish the cleanup. After all, we don't want our wonderful janitors to get overworked—they've got a big week coming up!"

"Hey, look!" said Robert, pointing past the marina piers.

Ben saw a tall sail and immediately recognized the sleek hull of the Jeanneau 57. The yacht was making for Cape Lee, sailing south.

Could Lyman have . . . ?

Turning quickly, Ben scanned the front of the school, and up on the third floor he spotted Lyman and Wally. They stood at the windows of Mrs. Hinman's room, looking southward.

Then Lyman lowered his gaze and saw Ben staring up at him.

They locked eyes, but just for a moment. Then Lyman did an odd thing. He raised a hand to his forehead and gave Ben a quick salute, navy style.

Almost involuntarily, Ben saluted him back, and Lyman turned and vanished.

"What was *that* about?" said Robert. He'd seen the whole thing.

"Not sure," said Ben.

That's what he told Gerritt.

But Ben knew exactly what those salutes meant.

It was like they were the captains of different ships, complimenting each other after a well-fought battle, recognizing a worthy opponent, a dangerous enemy.

The salutes meant something else as well.

Each of them knew that there would be another battle.

Soon.

KEEP A LOOKOUT FOR *We Hold These Truths,* THE 5TH AND FINAL BOOK IN THE BENJAMIN PRATT & THE KEEPERS OF THE SCHOOL SERIES

Also by Andrew Clements

Benjamin Pratt & the Keepers of the School

We the Children

Fear Itself

The Whites of Their Eyes

Big Al

Big Al and Shrimpy

Dogku

The Handiest Things in the World

A Million Dots

About Average

Extra Credit

Frindle

The Jacket

Jake Drake, Bully Buster

Jake Drake, Class Clown

Jake Drake, Know-It-All

Jake Drake, Teacher's Pet

The Janitor's Boy

The Landry News

The Last Holiday Concert

Lost and Found

Lunch Money

No Talking

The Report Card

Room One

The School Story

Troublemaker

A Week in the Woods